She looks as poised and controlling as she did when she turned her back on me for the last time, he thought, with a flicker of the falcon in his eyes. There had been little time to think over the past few days, but every second he'd been able to spare had overflowed with thoughts of her. Now he had come to a decision.

It was impossible to shut her out of his mind. He closed his hands slowly into fists. He had been away for too long, fighting through public battles and private negotiations. Now there was only one thing left to sort out. A provocative, priceless woman had trespassed into his private life, and tonight would see the showdown.

He ran a hand through his raven hair once more, and tried to pull his battle-weary uniform into some kind of order. Then he turned his ruthless stare back to the instrument panel. His mouth moved, and he almost smiled. At last. With one twitch of his hand he set his plane on the path down, to find the woman who could change his life for ever.

Christina Hollis was born in Somerset, and now lives in the idyllic Wye valley. She was born reading, and her childhood dream was to become a writer. This was realised when she became a successful journalist and lecturer in organic horticulture. Then she gave it all up to become a full-time mother of two and run half an acre of productive country garden.

Writing Mills & Boon® romances is another ambition realised. It fills most of her time, in between complicated rural school runs. The rest of her life is divided among garden and kitchen, either growing fruit and vegetables or cooking with them. Her daughter's cat always closely supervises everything she does around the home, from typing to picking strawberries!

You can learn more about Christina and her writing at www.christinahollis.com

Recent titles by the same author:

THE COUNT OF CASTELFINO
THE TUSCAN TYCOON'S PREGNANT HOUSEKEEPER
THE RUTHLESS ITALIAN'S INEXPERIENCED WIFE
HER RUTHLESS ITALIAN BOSS

WEIGHT OF THE CROWN

BY
CHRISTINA HOLLIS

First published in Great Britain 2011
by Mills & Boon, an imprint of Harlequin (UK) Limited,
Eton House, 18-24 Paradise Road, Richmond, Surrey TW9 1SR

© Christina Hollis 2011

ISBN: 978 0 263 22097 1

Harlequin (UK) policy is to use papers that are natural, renewable products and made from wood grown in sustainable forests. The logging and manufacturing process conform to the legal environmental regulations of the country of origin.

Printed and bound in Great Britain
by CPI Antony Rowe, Chippenham, Wiltshire

WEIGHT OF
THE CROWN

To Martyn, who makes all things possible.

PROLOGUE

LYSANDER was flying. Far below, the glitter of city lights was a diamond necklace drawn back into the velvet case of night. His lips parted in a wicked smile. He had made it to the top, and he was coming back to a hero's welcome. Nothing could stop him now, no matter how exhausted he was. His uniform was open at the neck, the sleeves turned back anyhow and he needed a shave. He dug the fingers of one hand through his tousled hair, trying to stop exhaustion shadowing his eyes. To him, tonight, sleep felt like a waste of time. He had too many things to do, and they all involved a certain person he hadn't seen for six days, four hours, eighteen minutes and counting…

Alyssa…

Her name moved around inside his mind like polished stones as he cruised over the sleeping English countryside. Several times his hand went towards his breast pocket as though to pull something out. Each time, he hesitated. His memory was enough. That snapshot couldn't affect him any more.

The intercom buzzed.

'You are cleared to land, Your Royal Highness!' a respectful voice informed him.

'That's OK.'

Lysander smiled. For the first time in his life, he felt comfortable with the title. Now he was flying through the night to reclaim what was his. This was what he was born to do. He had it all, and it felt good.

But the feeling didn't last.

His knuckles whitened as he gripped the controls of his private jet, anticipating trouble. It was a mistake to assume anything when it came to Alyssa. He didn't have everything he desired. Not yet.

That thought made him uneasy. Dragging at his cuff, he checked the watch on his smooth golden wrist. Timing this next move was crucial. He dug his teeth into his lower lip. The cause of all his sleepless nights would be in Ra'id's bedroom right now. Her changeless evening routine would be almost over. Everything would be peaceful, calm and predictable—until he dropped in.

Within seconds her neatly starched, ordered calm would be transformed into noisy chaos.

Lysander laughed. Adrenaline powered through his body, preparing him. The sort of happy homecoming he had dreamed about since he was a child was nearly within his grasp—but it wasn't guaranteed, not by any stretch of the imagination. He still had work to do. Alyssa Dene wasn't his—not yet. Lysander was a winner in his own country, but he had a different struggle in mind now. He was shaping up to confront Alyssa with what he had just done.

Lysander's mouth twitched as he considered the problem. This was going to be his hardest battle. He had already seen two tragedies in his thirty-two years, but there was not going to be a third. He was sure of that. So far things were going completely according to plan—*his* plan. But for how much longer?

His hand strayed towards his pocket again. With a sharp shake of his head, he slapped his fingers back to the controls. He was returning in triumph, secure in his position as leader of his country. He didn't want to spoil that. So the photograph stayed in his pocket, lodged like a cherry stone. He knew exactly how Miss Alyssa Dene would look right now, moving around the warm, welcoming rooms she had made her own. That was how he wanted to remember her right up to the end, whatever that might be.

His brow contracted. For the first time in his life, there was a slight chance things might not go entirely his way, but Lysander was determined. Thoughts of what he had done in the past, and how she had reacted to it, had tortured him for long enough. He was coming back to offer her the chance of a lifetime, whether she wanted it or not.

He felt his dark, strong features work with emotion, and resented it. That happened each time he remembered the angry words he had thrown at her on the night he left to secure the throne of Rosara.

I've *got nothing to prove!* You're *the one whose future is on the line…*

Lysander clenched his teeth until they ached. Snatching the damned photograph from his breast pocket, he slapped it down in front of him. As it came to rest on the instrument panel flesh and blood threatened to overwhelm him. All his best intentions crumbled to dust. When he looked at that picture, time stood still.

Suddenly it was summer in his heart again; his body and soul busy with thoughts of the woman whose presence could arouse him with desert-scorching fire. But then he had been forced to make a choice between his country, and her. She had turned her back on him, and the reason why would never go away. In the eyes of other people, Lysander was the world's most successful man. That was true—up until now. He had won the hearts of his people, but the only battle he truly cared about hadn't started yet. He exhaled heavily, trying to focus on the stellar image lying on the bulkhead before him. It was no good. He couldn't quite look her in the eyes.

Alyssa... He savoured her name as well as the sight of her tempting, toned body. The silky feel of her soft blonde hair between his fingers was such a distant dream, but this photograph brought it all back. That swimsuit was supposed to be discreet, but its sleek green gloss showed off her full breasts as provocatively as it sculpted her neat waist and warmly rounded hips.

Lysander drew in a slow, ragged breath. His hands could recognise her shape in the dark of a desert night, but the expression she wore in this picture chilled him to the bone.

She looks as poised and controlling as she did when she turned her back on me for the last time, he thought with a flicker of the falcon in his eyes. There had been little time to think over the past few days, but every second he could spare had overflowed with thoughts of her. Now he had come to a decision, and he was going to stick with it.

Lysander tried to concentrate on the instrument panel before him, not the image of a woman he had last heard telling him to go to hell. Working on automatic, he flicked switches and checked displays, but it was impossible to shut her out of his mind. He closed his hands slowly into fists around the controls. He had been away for too long, fighting through public battles and private negotiations. Now there was only one thing left to sort out. A provocative, priceless woman had trespassed into his private life, and tonight would see the showdown.

He ran a hand through his raven hair once more, and tried to pull his battle-weary uniform into some kind of order. Then he turned his ruthless stare back to the instrument panel. His mouth moved, and he almost smiled again. At last. With one twitch of his hand he set his plane on the path down to find the woman who could change his life for ever.

CHAPTER ONE

A month earlier.

THIS *is supposed to be fun*, Alyssa reminded herself. It should have been ideal. Everything she loved was all here in one place—solitude, a beautiful setting and time to think. The only downside was the weather. Raindrops were still rustling through the tree canopy after that last shower, but the sky was clearing. This was England in summer, after all. Changeable weather was all part of the *fun*.

She grimaced. That was the second time she had used the 'f' word inside thirty seconds, but it didn't make her feel any better. If only she could stop remembering... She shuddered.

Rebuilding some sort of existence for herself wasn't easy. This holiday was supposed to give her space and time to plan her future. Out here in the forest she had the room and the opportunity to think, but all she could do was brood on what had happened, instead of how she might move on.

She hugged her knees, trying to enjoy the feeling of being snug inside the entrance to her tent. It was hopeless. This sabbatical wasn't working. Listening to the gentle play of water welling up from the spring beside her, she shut her eyes and tried to clear her mind. This spot was a real find. It was miles off the beaten track, in a hidden valley that hadn't seen the hand of humans for years. There was wildlife, and flowers, and perfect peace—until her phone rang.

'Hi, it's only me.'

Alyssa tried her best to raise a smile. Karen, the agency manager, was a good friend, and that wasn't always a good thing. Today, it was part of the trouble.

'Look, please don't take this the wrong way, Karen, but I'd be glad if you could give me a bit of a break. I really don't need you to keep pushing work in my direction. I'm supposed to be getting away from the whole childcare scene for a bit.'

Looking back, there might have been the briefest of pauses, but Alyssa wasn't aware of it at the time.

'Who said this was a job offer?' her boss began breezily. 'I'm just ringing up to check that you're OK. Good grief, you thought I was calling to offer you the job that came in this morning? Believe me, you'll be glad you're *not* available when I tell you about it. They wanted the best, and they'll need it, but it's a poisoned chalice.'

Alyssa stiffened. 'It sounds like trouble.' Her mouth dried and she couldn't say any more.

'No, no. It's not as though the child is in actual *danger*...'

But the hint was there. Alyssa felt her blood run cold.

'So anyway, how do you feel, Alyssa? Any better?

What are you up to at the moment?' Karen said without pausing for breath.

'That doesn't matter. I'm more interested in that new job you mentioned. There's something wrong. I can hear it in your voice.'

'Rubbish! The new Regent of Rosara wants the best for his nephew. That's all.'

Alyssa gasped.

'That's *all*?'

Awful headlines had been splashed across every newspaper for days. To read about a child orphaned in a car crash while visiting his family's holiday home in England was bad enough. When A-list celebrity Lysander Kahani was named as his guardian, the story had stuck in Alyssa's mind. Glamorous Prince Lysander's link with the case had instantly snatched all the limelight from the little boy.

'The prince's people asked for you by name, Alyssa. You were recommended to them because they want the best, of course.'

'They'll need it, with that Casanova turning the poor child's home into an open house for idiots,' Alyssa muttered, her head full of all the lurid 'Playboy Gets Top Job' stories she had seen.

'But I'm going to tell them you aren't available,' Karen went on airily. 'Which is probably just as well for all concerned.'

Alyssa definitely didn't like the way the agency boss said that. 'Meaning?'

'Come off it, Lis, would you really want to work in a set-up like that? Everyone knows you're the best person in the world when it comes to taking care of children, but, let's face it, would you have been able to fit in with Prince Lysander's way of life? He's got such a terrible reputation, I knew you wouldn't want the job in a million years.'

Alyssa could feel herself being played, and she didn't like it, but she also couldn't deny it was working. Maybe this break was doing her some good after all. The only thing she had decided over the past few days was that her life had to change. Could this be where it started?

That child needed a calming influence in his life. Even in the midst of her own misery, Alyssa had never been able to ignore a child in need. Also, she had to admit to a faint flicker of curiosity—the first sign of life she'd felt for ages. What would the palace be like? How could she go about helping the little boy? *And after all*, she thought, *if I say I'm not available, they might go ahead and hire the first hopeless, brainless, wannabe celebrity they come across. Someone only interested in trailing the poor little boy around in Lysander's wake...*

That settled it for Alyssa.

'Have you actually put the royal family off yet, Karen?'

It was difficult to sound offhand when her heart was racing. Keeping quiet had wrecked her life before. And now, telling herself the only thing that mattered was what the child might be going through, she knew she had to have that job. She'd make sure little Ra'id Kahani was safe and properly looked after first, then worry about her own feelings afterwards.

'Not yet, no. I'm trying to find someone else for

them first. Telling them there *is* no one as good as you is the next thing on my "to do" list.'

'Then don't do it.' Alyssa plunged in before she had time to think about all the drawbacks. 'You don't need to ring them. I'll take the job, Karen,' she said with the blood pounding in her ears.

There was a considered silence at the other end of the line. Then her boss laughed. 'But what about the irresistible Prince Lysander? No woman is safe from his charm, apparently!'

'After what's happened to me over the past few months, I'm totally immune to men. Don't say you've forgotten one of the things that drove me to take this break from work in the first place.'

Karen hesitated. 'Of course…'

'Yes. Him.'

Jerry. Alyssa still couldn't bring herself to say the name out loud. Thinking about what that rat had done still made her feel ill. This Rosara job would be the perfect way to bury all her horrible memories. It would give her the new start she was craving so badly.

'So you think you can cope with a dark-eyed, dashing playboy?' The smile was obvious in Karen's voice.

'The only thing I'm interested in is his poor little nephew,' Alyssa said, and meant it. 'When can I start?'

'I'll tell them you're on your way.' Her boss laughed again.

Alyssa's nerve held right up until she reached the security checkpoint at the entrance to Combe House. She had worked for plenty of rich people in the past and was no stranger to being met by guards inside a home and at its doors, but never at gates so far from the house. It was a new experience for her. *But one I shall have to get used to,* she thought, driving towards the Kahanis' mansion along a curving drive that seemed to go on for ever. Starting with a new family always made her nervous, and these surroundings didn't do anything to make her feel better about the Kahani family. Untamed English woodland pressed in on all sides, while undergrowth spilled out over the gritty approach road. *They're probably nocturnal,* she thought grimly. *And too busy partying all night to care what the place looks like to daytime visitors.*

As she drove on, a huge rambling mansion rose out of the undergrowth ahead of her. Combe House had turrets, weathervanes and flagpoles, all lichenous with age. She could hardly take it all in. It was the most beautiful house she had ever seen, and the setting was lovely despite the weeds.

This whole place is like something out of Sleeping Beauty! she thought.

A little knot of sharp-suited security men stood chatting beside the great entrance doors to the house. When Alyssa rolled down her window to ask where she should park, she got a first taste of working for Lysander Kahani. One man took her car keys to save her the trouble of parking, while a second escorted her into the building. He showed her into a waiting room the size of a ballroom. Much of it was hidden beneath dust sheets while the delicate plaster details of cornices and dados could be restored, but the parts that had been finished were truly beautiful. Alyssa hoped it would take the Combe House staff a long time to find anyone to deal with her. She wanted a chance to look around the room on her own, first.

She didn't get it. An awful racket bowled through the house towards her. It was a lot of people jabbering among themselves, seasoned with the sound of ringing mobile phones.

The Kahani state circus was coming to town.

Alyssa checked her appearance in the nearest mirror, but she needn't have bothered. A cavalcade of smartly dressed staff burst into the room where she was waiting, but showed no sign of noticing her. They were only interested in the tall, lean man who strode ahead of them. He had the look of an avenging angel, while they clamoured for his attention like a nest of ravens. Common sense told Alyssa this figure must be Lysander Kahani, but it was hard to recognise him. This man didn't look much like the amused playboy prince pictured in all the celebrity magazines, and on the front pages of all the newspapers. He looked angry, dark hair tousled untidily over his brow, and he wore a perfectly fitted light grey business suit rather than the tuxedo of his photos. His tie was missing, and his plain white shirt was open at the neck. He certainly wasn't smiling, and there was a dangerous gleam in his eyes as he saw her watching him. Despite the crowd and noise, Alyssa had never felt so alone and vulnerable.

I thought the royal family were here on holiday, but you'd never know from Prince Lysander's expression, she thought.

While his rapier gaze was distracted by the arrival of yet another electronic message, she tried to study her new employer. Lysander Kahani was a six-and-a-half-foot scowl, his height impressive and intimidating, but she could only bring herself to look at the lower seventy inches or so. To make up for that, she studied him all the way up from his highly polished, handmade shoes to his dark shaded chin, and then down again. It was scarily enjoyable—so she did it again. On the return journey her eyes made their way right up to his. As she tried her best to look cool and unapproachable she saw the anger leave his face.

As his eyes locked onto hers, he spoke sharply to his crowd of followers. Alyssa didn't speak his language, but his words had a questioning lilt that was easy enough to understand. He must want to know who she was, and why she was there. His staff all fell silent and turned to stare at her as if she were another exhibit for their madhouse. Alyssa tried to concentrate on the blurry newspaper photos of the poor little boy, Prince Ra'id, who had lost both his parents and must have been shoved aside in favour of this mob. Folding her hands in front of her as a defence, she took a deep breath.

'I am Alyssa Dene. I'm here by special request of Prince Lysander of Rosara, because I'm to be his nephew's new nanny.'

The words came out louder and more haughtily than she intended. Before she could apologise, something changed in Lysander Kahani's expression. It softened, and in the face of his dark amusement Alyssa stopped thinking straight. She couldn't help it. The sight of his smile sent all the questions she had lined up for her new employer scattering like beads on a tray. It was obvious he knew the effect he was having on her. This was more fun to him than work. His taut frame relaxed. With a few words he sent his horde of advisors scuttling away. Tossing the sheaf of paperwork he was holding onto the nearest table, Lysander followed them to the door and closed it behind them. As he leaned back against it Alyssa came to her senses. She was now totally alone with a notorious man. If that weren't bad enough, somehow in the past few seconds he had become more attractive than he appeared in all his photographs put together.

She tried to speak, but no sound came out. Lysander Kahani showed every sign of revelling in the situation.

'That's more like it!' he said in beautifully accented English. 'Now I can hear myself think, and devote my whole attention to you. This job is playing havoc with my lifestyle, I can tell you.'

Alyssa swallowed hard as he prowled towards her. His wicked smile sent tremors straight through her body. It felt incredible, but she couldn't afford to enjoy it. A man without a fraction of Lysander's charm had wrecked her life only a few months ago, and she was still trying to recover. Every ounce of her common sense told her this was a dangerous situation and she ought to resist, but Lysander was looking at her as though she were the only woman in the world. The expression in his rich brown, dark-lashed eyes made it difficult not to give in and simply revel in the wonderful feeling of being admired.

'D-don't you think you'd better deal with all that paperwork first, Prince Lysander?' She faltered, looking at the chaos scattered over the nearest table top.

She was suddenly desperate for more time to prepare herself for this encounter.

'No, I don't,' he said, strolling over to position himself between her and the table. By leaning back against it he hid the heap of work from her, but she had already stopped looking at it. The fine lines of his suit and the long, strong fingers he curled over the edge of the table top had captured her attention. 'It's only parcels of trouble, tied up in red tape. Forget it. I'd much rather talk to you...*Alyssa.*'

The way he purred her name sent a shiver of anticipation across her sensitised skin. She was already nervous about starting work for such an infamous man, and his flirting set new butterflies dancing inside her tummy. The last thing she needed was this handsome stranger taking over her body by stealth before she was safely hidden away in Combe House's nursery wing. She had to show she meant business right away.

'It—it might be important, Your Royal Highness.'

'You'd like to think so, wouldn't you?' His well-shaped mouth twisted with the sulky retort. 'Maybe if it was about the important things in life I could raise some enthusiasm, but it's nothing but CRB checks, Health & Safety issues and risk assessments concerning a child I don't even know. But why are we talking about all that, when we could be talking about *you*?'

His annoyance over something so close to her heart was the wake-up call Alyssa needed. She stopped melting in the warmth of his gaze and fastened her new employer with a look of her own.

'Because I am your nephew's new nanny, and right now that paperwork *is* the most important thing—in *his* life.' *You self-centred drone!* she added silently to herself.

Prince Lysander Kahani stopped smiling, and she felt a brief spark of satisfaction. That was quickly extinguished as his dark eyes continued to ripple over her like a caress.

'You sound like a woman who knows what she's doing and have the added advantage of looking nothing like a headmistress. Goodbye, all my thoughts of a terrifying harridan, and hello to the beautiful vision that is Miss Alyssa Dene!'

With a ridiculously extravagant gesture, he reached out for her hand. Lifting it to his lips, he brushed her fingers with a kiss of long, slow meaning.

'Please don't do that, Your Royal Highness,' Alyssa said sternly, forcing herself to pull her hand out of his grasp, but unable to stop the corners of her mouth curling up at his teasing.

He gave her a mock pained look. 'Don't spoil my one moment of hope, Alyssa. You are my only ray of sunshine—the first woman below the rank of minister I've been alone with in over three weeks. Look at me!' He groaned, throwing up his arms in mock despair. 'I used to have a life. Now I'm a caged tiger, performing for the benefit of others.'

Alyssa was transfixed—a rabbit trapped in the headlights of his charm. Catching herself gazing at him, she shook her head as though waking from a dream. Angry with his effect on her, she gave a dramatic sigh and said:

'Cursed with a fortune and forced to live in a place

like this? Dear, dear—it must be absolute *hell* for you, Your Royal Highness!'

The moment the words popped out, Alyssa knew she should have kept her mouth shut. Lysander's eyes hardened to jet. The change in him was like the sun going behind a thundercloud.

Why the hell did I say that? He may be an arrogant so-and-so, but he's still royalty! What will happen to his poor little nephew if I get sacked before I've even met the child?

'In the past month I've lost my brother, my sister-in-law, and my freedom.' Lysander Kahani's voice was as cold as the shiver running through Alyssa's body.

There was nothing for it but to apologise. 'I know—and I'm sorry, Your Royal Highness, but my first loyalty is to little Ra'id——' she burst out.

'I can see that, by the way you didn't let me finish what I was saying,' he cut in smoothly. 'I was going on to tell you that picking up the pieces my brother left behind is a full-time job. It shouldn't leave me any time for self-pity.' He gave the tiniest nod of acknowledgement, and the hint of a wry smile.

Alyssa didn't like the way he interrupted her, but at least he understood why she had spoken out.

'At least when I take charge of your poor little nephew it will be one weight off your shoulders.'

His gaze had been working its way down her body with slow enjoyment, but her words stopped him. He dragged his attention back to her face. 'You say that as though you actually give a damn, Miss Alyssa Dene.'

'That's because I do. I'm here to make sure your

nephew is properly looked after, and gets a sensible upbringing.'

'And to bring a little light into my life while you do it,' he said with a widening smile. 'You can start by dropping the formalities. As we'll be working so closely together, call me Lysander.'

Alyssa hesitated. This was quite a normal request from an employer, but with a smooth operator like Lysander Kahani it might be an intimacy too far. It broke down a barrier between them, and that couldn't be a good idea. She already knew it was desperately important to keep this man at arm's length, so he couldn't affect her judgement. That had failed her in the past, when it came to adults. The only thing she wanted to rush into now was little Prince Ra'id's nursery. If she couldn't trust herself, how could she trust a womaniser like Lysander? Only thoughts of the poor child involved stopped her making some sort of excuse and escaping from Combe House while she still could. Good or bad, this man was her new employer. She had to develop a working relationship with him, and that would involve some give and take.

'All right, then…Lysander. You can trust me to look after poor Prince Ra'id as if he was my own child,' she told him.

He raised his dark, finely arched brows. 'There speaks a woman who's never met him!'

'I'm here to care for your poor little nephew, Lysander, not your feelings. So while I'm sorry about your family bereavement and the way you've been forced into becoming Prince Regent, you and I have to work together to make the best of it, for little Ra'id's sake,' she said firmly, hoping she could be equally determined when it came to resisting Lysander's charm.

'Nobody's ever said anything like that to me before, either.'

The crease between his brows deepened.

Alyssa realised a man would never have risked saying something like that to Prince Lysander Kahani. Only a woman could get away with it. She allowed herself the hint of a smile. Lysander's interest in her body was turning out to have advantages as well as danger. It could deflect his anger—at least for the moment.

'Then I hope I can keep your nephew a bit more down to earth.'

Lysander was beginning to have doubts about her. She could see it in his face.

'I wish you luck,' he murmured. 'As Ra'id is my brother's son, I've seen him now and again over the years, but that's all. What I've heard about him from his nursery maids is bad enough. It'll be a brave woman who refuses that child anything, from the sound of it.'

When she didn't laugh, he shrugged and stuck his hands in his pockets. 'Well…if you feel confident enough to make a mad claim like that, the least I can do is match it, and raise you. What can I do to help you in your hopeless task, and earn your undying gratitude when I've done it?'

She raised her eyebrows, then met his question with one of her own.

'How do you get on with Ra'id?'

He responded with a quizzical smile. 'Me? I don't. My family has used this house in England as a bolt hole for years, so we've met up here regularly for holidays, but that doesn't mean I've had anything to do with the child.'

I might have guessed, Alyssa thought. 'So you're quite happy to leave that poor mite completely in the hands of strangers?'

His expression hardened. 'Of course, when they come with qualifications and references like yours. What else would you expect me to do? I don't know the first thing about children.'

'Lysander!' Alyssa chided him, but it was only when she took a step backwards and away from him to underline her disapproval that he looked at all bothered.

Annoyed at her reaction, he moved towards an intercom on the desk. 'Ra'id has been well looked after by the general nursery staff here since his last nanny left. I think. At least, I assume... No, I'm sure that's been the case,' he said through gritted teeth.

Alyssa could tell that not knowing annoyed him. That was a detail she could work with.

'Well, you'll be able to judge that side of things for yourself when I've called someone to take you to the nursery,' he went on irritably.

Alyssa had other ideas. 'I'd rather you took me yourself, Lysander. After all, you did ask how you could help,' she said, and this time her smile was as winning as any of the looks he kept turning on her.

CHAPTER TWO

THEY were tempting words, but Alyssa's body language belied her inviting smile, and warned Lysander. He knew she was only trying to use his reputation against him again. Liking her cheek, however, he escorted her to the nursery with the indulgent smile of a man who always got what he wanted. Women generally fell into his arms within seconds, and Alyssa was the first woman in a long while to present him with anything like a challenge. Her beautiful body and long, shapely legs made this new experience very enjoyable. He was confident she would soon be running to him for comfort, and for a prize like that he was willing to be patient. Little Ra'id had sent plenty of distressed nursery maids his way over the past few weeks. Miss Alyssa Dene was different, there was no doubt about that, but Lysander was sure he only had to wait for this latest peach to fall into his lap.

As they walked he sent a series of covert glances in her direction and liked what he saw. She was tall for a woman, so the crown of her head was almost level with his shoulder. Her feminine curves were in perfect proportion, and her blue-eyed beauty was topped by a swirl of shining blonde hair. He knew exactly how that

silken waterfall would feel when he released it from
her prissy French plait, and looked forward to doing
it.

They went straight to the nursery wing's dining
room, drawn by an unholy racket. It was full of people,
all talking at once. Lysander introduced Alyssa, then
stood back. The crowd fell silent. The staff, like him,
were watching to see what Alyssa would do when confronted with five-year-old Ra'id. The child was holding court at the head of his dining table and scowling
like a little old man. When Lysander saw the peculiar
collection of food on the table, he frowned, too. None
of it looked edible—especially the sardines in chocolate sauce and the cupcakes spread with Marmite. He
watched Alyssa sum up the situation. Then he leaned
in to enjoy the fragrant sensation of whispering into
her small, perfectly formed ear.

'Meet the poor little orphaned mite you're going to
rescue from his wicked, uncaring uncle.'

He expected her to apologise for her starchy attitude
towards him, but she didn't. Instead she hissed, 'He
seems to have recovered from the tragedy well enough
to have your staff on the run!'

'That's because he was about as close to his parents
as I was to mine,' Lysander flashed back.

She gave him a strange look, then pinned on a smile
before speaking out loud to the infant dictator.

'Good afternoon, Prince Ra'id. It doesn't look as
though traditional Rosarian food meets with your approval, so we'll get rid of it, *and* all these people.'

'But he hasn't had any food yet!' A shocked voice
burst out from the crowd. 'And it isn't traditional—we've

brought him everything he asked for, but nothing's been good enough yet.'

'That's a shame,' Alyssa said evenly. 'But lunchtime should have been over a long time ago.'

'I'm hungry!' Ra'id said through clenched teeth.

The huddle of servants held its breath. Lysander carried on lazily watching Alyssa. She took no notice of her little charge. Instead, she started piling up plates with quick, neat movements. After an exchange of glances, the rest of the staff stepped forward to help her. In minutes the table was clear and the room empty apart from Lysander, Alyssa and the little boy.

'I'm hungry!' Ra'id repeated, this time with more of a whine.

'No, you aren't. If you'd been hungry, you would have eaten the first thing you were served. You're not to treat your staff like that, Prince Ra'id. They spent a lot of time satisfying your demands, so the least you could have done was try something. As your uncle Lysander has just told you, I'm in charge now. From today, you'll eat at regular times. Whatever arrives is what you'll eat, and that's an end to it. There will be *no* alternatives.' She glanced at her watch, then looked at Lysander. 'Do you eat high tea at Combe House?'

'For you, Alyssa, anything is possible.' He chuckled.

'Then could you order a simple meal of egg on toast for His Majesty, to be served in your dining room in half an hour?'

'I don't like egg. What is it?' the little boy piped up.

'It's what you're having for tea,' Alyssa said with

a determination Lysander wished he could see more often.

Ra'id wasn't so impressed. 'No! And I can do what I like, because I'm King.'

Lysander had consoled enough nursery maids to know that was the killer line. It always worked. He glanced at Alyssa with a grin that said *I'd like to see you get out of that!*

Alyssa didn't need to answer him. She knelt down beside Ra'id and folded her arms on the ruined surface of his miniature Georgian dining table so that her face was very close to his.

'Oho—-not yet, you aren't! Listen to me, young man. Your uncle Lysander is going to be in charge of you, and everything else around you, for at least the next four thousand days, so what he says, goes. That's a long time, so get used to it. And he says you'll eat the lovely food the staff are kind enough to make for you. If you don't, you'll go hungry.' She looked up at Lysander with battle blazing in her eyes. 'Right?'

Wide-eyed and speechless, the little boy switched his gaze from Alyssa to Lysander, searching for support.

'That's right, isn't it, Lysander?' Alyssa repeated, more forcefully this time.

Lysander knew she wanted him to back her up, but he took his time. He was busy with his own thoughts, enjoying the arousal that pulsed through his body as he watched this determined and beautiful woman in action. The sensation was far more enjoyable than talking to her about nursery routine. Miss Alyssa Dene had the sort of nerve he had never encountered before. He already knew she wasn't going to roll over and submit to him like so many women that had filled his universe until now. He would have to break down her resistance to him inch by inch. It was an idea he found intensely exciting. It would make the moment she finally fell under his spell a real triumph, and a conquest worthy of his maverick skills. He allowed a slow, seductive smile to warm his face. Her need for him was so deeply buried she might not recognise it yet, but she would. Given time. He would make sure of it.

'Right...' He teased the word out slowly. 'So from now on, Ra'id, you'll do everything Alyssa tells you, OK?'

His answer satisfied her, although she laid down the law to Ra'id for a long time after that. While she rattled on, Lysander lost himself again in more luscious thoughts involving silk sheets, perfumed massage oil and Miss Alyssa Dene's soft curves. He only realised he should have been listening to her instead when she coughed politely to attract his attention.

'So, Lysander, Ra'id and I will see you in your dining room in half an hour.'

'Of course,' Lysander said suavely, still wondering if she knew what she was letting herself in for. He sent another leisurely glance over her body. The tempting reality of her promised to be even better than his fantasy.

'Miss Alyssa Dene is the best nanny in the business, Ra'id,' he told his nephew. 'And I'm looking forward to discovering what other talents she has, very soon.' He smiled, tilting his head towards her in a way that never failed to soften women. She stared at him, her cool blue eyes as assured as his own technique.

'It's a pity smiling doesn't seem to be one of them,' he went on, standing back to give her room to melt over his teasing. It had no effect.

'Childcare isn't a laughing matter, Lysander.'

Her wide-set eyes would have been beautiful if they hadn't been focusing a stare on him that was as hard as sapphires.

The last few weeks had stretched Lysander's patience so thin, it was practically transparent. He heard himself snap, like an elastic band that had been stretched too far.

'Then that's a shame. You'll need a sense of humour if you're going to work here.'

He regretted it instantly. Unleashing his bitterness wasn't the way to win over rebellious women. Stepping in close to her again, he softened his retort by patting her gently on the back. 'If only to put up with my short temper. So if you wouldn't mind giving me a few moments of your time outside so we can discuss it, Nanny—?'

His hand slid sensuously over her ribcage on its way to become a support under her elbow.

'My name is Alyssa!'

She jerked away from him so savagely, Ra'id gave a little cry of alarm. Instantly, she swooped down to comfort the little boy. Any angry remarks Lysander might have made at her overreaction died on his lips when he saw the way she reassured his nephew—that, and the way her shirt gaped a little as she bent forward. It gave him an illicit glimpse of her lacy bra as it cupped the creamy swell of her breasts. The view was so delicious, he forgave her everything.

It made him look forward to seeing a whole lot more of her, very soon.

Alyssa used a combination of psychology and her own novelty value to make tea a triumph. Comfort eating over the past few months had made her staid navy-blue nanny's uniform a bit snug. This worked wonders on Lysander. She had his full attention, although it did tend to gravitate towards her breasts. To get him back on track she told him his good manners and charm would soon rub off on his nephew. Ra'id turned out to have a big appetite, and he was so astonished that anyone would stand up to him, he was easy to manage. Food was the perfect bribe. All Alyssa had to do was to make sure he got a healthy diet, and by keeping Lysander on side she would have all the backup she needed.

She was still smiling hours later as she left Ra'id's bedroom that evening. She closed the door so quietly, it didn't make a sound. She could have laughed with relief at the end of such an exhausting, perfect day, but didn't want to wake her little charge. These first few hours in her new job had achieved what her holiday had failed to do—distracted her from the past and helped her to move into the future. It turned out she'd needed a new challenge, and she was relishing it. Ra'id was a real handful, but that was because no one had cared enough to teach him how to behave properly—until now. He was quick, clever, and underneath he had the makings of a dear little chap. Now she could relax for a few hours, and thank her lucky stars that she had gone with her instincts rather than her emotions. She had taken this position to save Ra'id from falling into the hands of some wage slave who was only interested in what the job prospects were. Now she was looking after him, everything would be fine. The only fly in the ointment was her unprecedented response to Lysander, but what with her past and his present she'd certainly never be silly enough to give into him—however wickedly tempting his smile might be…

As she entered the suite's sitting room she jumped violently when she saw that the object of her thoughts had made himself at home on one of the nursery's low couches, his long legs stretched out beneath a table. A tray set for two with fine china and a steaming cafetiere waited in front of him, untouched. A dozen downlighters around the walls gave the room a soft golden glow.

'Thank you, Lysander.' Alyssa kept her voice cool and professional, desperate not to show him how much his presence unsettled her. She preferred speaking to children rather than adults, but talking with Lysander was all too easy. She tried to concentrate on tidying the room, hoping her busyness would hide her nerves. 'When you told me you never normally had anything to do with Ra'id, I thought it meant you didn't have any interest in him. It was good of you to sit with us while he had tea in the main dining room. The different surroundings made him a bit uncertain, and that really helped him behave. Eating with you and other adults instead of being waited on alone will really help his manners. You'll be a great example for him to follow.

Is there any chance you could make afternoon tea with him a regular thing?'

'It'll be my pleasure, as long as you promise to always be there, too,' Lysander purred.

The room's low light gave his aristocratic features a shadowy mystery—but there was no mistaking the meaning in his eyes. During the meal they had all taken together Alyssa had been focused on Ra'id, but that couldn't stop her feeling the warmth of Lysander's interest. Alone with him now, she felt coils of attraction snake through her body. Tearing herself away from his gaze, she moved methodically around the room, picking up scattered toys and plumping cushions.

'You must have given your army of attendants the slip,' she said without looking at him.

'I told them to leave me, yes,' he said in a light, conversational way.

Remember, men like him gain your confidence, then abandon you when you're at your most vulnerable. That's how it works, Alyssa told herself firmly.

When the room was as neat as it was going to get, she couldn't think of anything else to do to avoid his eyes except pouring the coffee. Trying not to let her nervousness show, she approached the table from the opposite side to where he sat. As she reached for the handle of the cafetiere his hand closed in on hers and he lifted it out of her grasp.

'That's OK. I'll pour the coffee. You should sit down and relax, Alyssa. It's been a busy day for you. And for me, too. You've given me plenty to think about.'

Until that moment Alyssa had been careful to keep her eyes on the tray, but that made her look up and question him. He was watching her with the exotic look of a well fed panther.

It's bound to be some sort of line, but there's nothing to worry about as long as I keep that thought in mind, she told herself.

'What do you mean?'

'The way you improved Ra'id's behaviour right from the start, by laying down strict boundaries for him. That impressed me. I went back to my staff and put some ground rules of my own in place, to make my life more structured. My nicely pampered, trouble-free life, as you were quick to point out,' he drawled, smiling at her in a way calculated to melt the stoniest heart.

Alyssa tried to resist, but the crafty way he recalled their first meeting started every muscle in her face working as she tried to avoid returning his smile.

'I'd hate to be followed around by all those people the whole time.'

'I do. But that's the way my brother worked, and having all those staff hounding me from day one hadn't given me enough time to devise a better system. I think better when I'm on my own. Clearing my mind by sending them all away for a while gave me the chance to work out a sensible routine for myself. And all it took was the sight of you, taking control.' He lifted one of the little black and gold cups of coffee towards her. 'Cream and sugar?'

'Cream, please. That's all.' She felt suddenly shy, rather than scared of him.

'I prefer cappuccino myself.'

'Oh, so do I!' They both looked surprised at her quick reply, and then smiled.

'You and I will have to indulge ourselves one day,' Lysander said. 'My late brother thought frothy coffee was undignified, and out of keeping with high office.' His smile had been getting wider by the second and Alyssa couldn't resist its power any longer. She could feel her own face relaxing, too.

'Thoughts like that don't stop you?'

'Nothing stops me.' His voice was warm.

Alyssa didn't doubt it. She leaned back in her seat, trying to make the point that she didn't intend starting anything.

'This is very good coffee. Your brother may have had a point. I've heard he was very respectable. When you can drink coffee that tastes like this, why risk pushing any boundaries?' she said, making it clear she didn't only mean coffee.

Lysander wasn't about to be put off so easily. 'Akil didn't start laying down the law until he was unlucky in love and then *bang*! He reverted to the family type where many things were concerned. For one thing, when it came to women he decided they should be seen and not heard—and preferably not seen either.' He gave her another smile. 'I get the feeling you'd be happy to keep this nursery wing as your own private space. I suspect he would have approved of you.'

'All I'm interested in is giving his son a good start in life.' Glowing with quiet pride, Alyssa took another sip of her coffee. 'It's the early days yet, but I think I'm going to like it here. I already love working with Ra'id so much, I'll be quite happy to fit in with whatever you want, Lysander.'

The moment the words left her lips Alyssa went hot

all over. It was exactly the wrong thing to say to a dangerously tempting man like this.

'That's what I like to hear.' He laughed.

'Just remember, I'm not here for your benefit!'

Lysander was so taken aback by her sharp retort, Alyssa had time to organise her thoughts before carrying on.

'My interest is in children, and making sure they're properly looked after. From what I understand, Ra'id has suffered all his life from a high turnover among his carers, so I intend sticking with this job for as long as I'm needed. That's *needed*, and not *wanted*, Lysander,' she said with chilling emphasis, letting him know that she assumed infidelity ran through his veins. 'I'm not going to let anything affect the way I care for Ra'id. That's why I want to get one thing clear from the start. There have to be ground rules for us as well as him.'

He slipped her a sidelong glance. Alyssa's heartbeat accelerated, but she tried to ignore her pounding pulse.

'I mean it.'

'That's a shame, but I suppose I should have guessed.' He sighed, then took a long drink of coffee. 'I've seen for myself how seriously you take your work. Does this mean you think sex isn't a laughing matter, either?'

Alyssa swallowed, knowing she had to dodge his question. Every time she looked at Lysander she noticed some new detail about him. The slight natural curl in his dark hair, or the muscles that were hardly concealed by the fine fabric of his crisp white shirt.

'It really doesn't matter what I think about anything, except my job,' she said, with a determination to ignore his smile. 'I'm employed to care for Ra'id. You've got your work cut out caring for his country, Lysander. We both want the same thing.' She felt embarrassed about exactly how true that was, and knew she was colouring up again. It was a good job the background lighting was so soft. It hid her embarrassment as well as her feelings. 'And that's the best thing for Ra'id. It means you and I have to work together as a team, and I mean *work*.' She emphasised the last word carefully.

'And I have no doubt at all that we will,' he drawled, making Alyssa wonder what he thought of as work. 'That's why I'm going to study your methods as closely as I can. The job of Regent of Rosara couldn't be more different from the life I've lived until now. With Ra'id years away from becoming King, and despite my brother's best attempts at marrying me off, I'm still his only living relative. That means our country's succession is in a precarious state. I have to make sure nothing happens to Ra'id, while running Rosara at the same time, and I intend to succeed at both jobs.'

Alyssa saw he was deadly serious, and knew she had underestimated him. 'That's a real challenge.'

'I know, but I specialise in those.'

She had been thinking so hard about how a playboy was going to juggle two jobs like that, she didn't realise he had been leaning steadily closer and closer to her. When he laid a hand on her arm, she jumped.

'That's why I need your help, Alyssa.'

She pulled her arm away smartly. 'If there's anything I can do to help Ra'id, I will. But that's all, Lysander.'

'Of course. You've made your point, so I'll make

mine. I prefer partnerships of pleasure.' Despite her obvious anger, he didn't sound at all apologetic.

'I suppose by that you mean little and often,' Alyssa snapped.

The smile returned to his beautiful mouth. 'I've never had any complaints.'

'Until you met me, and I'm out of bounds,' she told him meaningfully. 'As long as you remember that, Lysander, you can keep your record with women—which I'm sure must be one hundred per cent perfect.'

'Oh, don't worry. One little setback in a lifetime wouldn't bother me. A single rejection among thousands of triumphs would only amount to a fraction of a percentage point,' he said with a careless smile.

'Ah, but if you don't try, you'll make *sure* you never fail—'

Alyssa had never known a man with such easy, natural charm. Those flashing eyes and that devilish smile made him almost impossible to resist, but then she remembered something. His one and only weakness would always be her greatest strength.

'And if you ever force me to give you a black eye, Lysander, it would make other girls think twice about tangling with you, until your bruises have faded.'

He stopped smiling. His eyes narrowed. He pursed his lips, thinking.

'I'm a fast healer, but…point taken.'

Alyssa wasn't going to take any chances. 'I'm serious, Lysander.'

He took another long, slow sip of coffee but his eyes didn't once leave her face. 'I'm sure you are.'

'I'm here to work, so I don't have time for

distractions. I couldn't live with myself if I didn't do my very best for your little prince. I once let a child down...' She paused, not wanting to complete the story. 'From that moment on, my job became the most important thing in my life. Do you understand?'

Lysander leaned back, resting one arm along the back of the couch. His eyes were dark and inscrutable. 'Ah...yes, I remember somebody bringing that to my attention when they were checking your references. It was truly a tragedy that that little boy died because nobody took any notice when you told them how sick he was. That was unforgivable.'

Alyssa's heart began to beat very quickly, and not only because of the way he was studying her. Talking to Jerry about the tragedy of little Georgie had been hard enough. Discussing it with a stranger would be impossible.

'Yes, it was. Which is why I'd rather you changed the subject,' she said abruptly, her breathing shallow.

Lysander's expression altered. The intensity of his gaze made her blush.

I was never this forceful until—she thought, and felt the sharp pain of sadness in her throat. *Oh, no. Why must that come back to haunt me, right now?* The events of a few months ago had snowballed until they threatened to suck all the life out of her. This job was her chance of a fresh start. She couldn't afford to weaken.

Lysander was so self-confident. Alyssa wished she had his sort of nerve, but she was at least determined not to let him see her eyes fill with tears. She looked away quickly, but for the first time since she had lost

Georgie she found that her tears were easily blinked away. Painfully, she wondered if this was the start of her recovery.

'Of course. It's no wonder you mistrust people after that.' Lysander's voice was as slow and calculated as his smile. 'Is there anything I can do to persuade you we aren't all bad?'

He had picked up on her suspicions about him, so there was no point in denying them. It wasn't good for her new employer to feel he was under surveillance, but that wasn't Alyssa's only worry. If a gorgeous man like this could see how troubled she was, her life really had gone too far in the wrong direction. She had to do something, fast, but what? Maybe she *could* do with talking about what had happened rather than bottling everything up…but this handsome, piratical prince looked more trouble than he was worth. Wanting to talk was one thing. Trusting him was something else. Finishing her coffee, she put her cup and saucer back on the tray and stood up.

'Well, thank you for the drink, but unless you have some aspect of Ra'id's care you'd like to discuss I think you'd better go, Lysander. I've got a lot to do.' She took a last look around the sitting room, then started off towards the door she assumed must lead to her own suite. 'The chap who parked my car earlier said he'd bring my luggage up but I got so involved with Ra'id, I haven't even had a chance to find where I'm sleeping.'

'The nanny's rooms are through there.' He pointed to the door. 'But that way is kept locked all the time, to stop Ra'id disturbing her during the night. You'll have to go out into the corridor and use the main door, at the top of the stairs.'

Alyssa flashed a dangerous look at him. 'And how would you know that, if you've never had anything to do with Ra'id before?'

Lysander smiled at her knowingly. 'Let's call it a lucky guess, shall we?'

'Well, the minute I find the key I'm going to unlock that door, and leave it open. That's how it's going to stay. I can assure you I'll never have any reason to stop Ra'id coming into my rooms to see me.'

'Really?' He gave her a mocking look of disbelief.

'Really.'

Her reply led him to give a casual shrug. 'Then it must be time for me to take you to your lonely suite.'

Alyssa raised her eyebrows.

'To the door and no further,' he assured her, offering his arm.

She hesitated. All day she had fought against falling under his spell. She had managed it so far. Surely she could reward herself with this one, brief point of contact? The fear that Lysander would misunderstand and assume it was the start of something warred with the excitement of being escorted by such a gorgeous, polite man. She already knew he was too much temptation, but had to find out if he was enough of a gentleman.

'Thanks, but I want you to know I'm giving you the benefit of some very big doubts, Lysander,' she told him, slipping her hand into the crook of his arm.

It was just as well she answered before the sensation of his warm, vital body rose through the thin fabric of his jacket. The feel of it shook Alyssa to the core.

She wanted to go on standing there in the middle of the room, enjoying the casual intimacy with this dark stranger. Lysander had other ideas. At the very moment she was most vulnerable, he ignored his advantage and started off towards the door.

'Would it help to put your mind at rest about me if we talked about work?' he asked her.

'That depends,' Alyssa said warily. 'Whose work did you want to discuss? Yours or mine?'

'Yours, of course. Now I've discovered little Ra'id isn't the creature from hell that everyone warned me about, I think I will want to take a more active role in his upbringing.'

Alyssa considered his words carefully. Ra'id was so full of himself, he wouldn't be helped by a fickle uncle who would be distracted by every woman who lured him away. On the other hand, whatever his motives, she didn't want to put Lysander off getting closer to Ra'id. In her bitter experience, it was better to have an adult getting in her way than taking no interest, and ignoring her professional advice.

'You've already told me that Ra'id didn't have a very close relationship with his parents. What he needs is some stability and routine in his life, not to mention some love and affection from a parent figure. If you could offer him that, it would be great. I'd love to have your help,' she continued cautiously, 'although I wouldn't want you to overcommit yourself. Why don't you try to make tea time with Ra'id a daily appointment to begin with, and see how you manage with that? Making some time available regularly in your schedule is much better than overwhelming him with attention to begin with, and then leaving him high and dry when something comes up to divert your attention.'

'I agree. I can't abide people who promise everything and then don't deliver.'

Alyssa looked at him quickly. 'That sounded heartfelt!'

'I've got good reason,' he told her, but didn't say anything else until they reached a door at the point where the nursery wing joined the main house.

'Here it is—the main entrance to your suite. To the door and no further, as promised.'

'Thank you—and I didn't promise anything at all, so that means you won't be disappointed when I say goodbye and let you go,' Alyssa said firmly, taking her hand from his arm. Going inside her suite, she turned around quickly to block the doorway in case he tried to follow her.

'I was thinking about someone else who didn't keep their word—to me.' His voice was slow and thoughtful. 'I find this hard to say but the fact is I need you, Alyssa.'

Alarmed, she took another step backwards into her rooms and tried to close the door on him. Lysander was too quick for her, and grabbed the edge of the door. 'I didn't mean to upset you, Alyssa. For once, I wasn't flirting. I meant that I need you *professionally*, because I don't know the first thing about children.'

He sounded so genuinely pained, she laughed. 'You were one yourself once, don't forget!'

'I know and I remember all too well what I had to go through. I admit, I'd rather leave all the caring to experts like you, and just be there for the fun stuff,' he said with real feeling.

Alyssa was moved. Without realising what she was doing, she reached out and patted him on the arm.

'That's better than nothing, and right now might be exactly what Ra'id needs his uncle for. It'll be great.'

'With you in charge, I'm sure it will be perfect.' His voice was a low murmur, full of possibilities. Alyssa tensed, but his hand slid from the door straight into his pocket.

For two heartbeats she thought about simply closing the door on him, but she couldn't do it. Lysander didn't move a muscle. His stillness was as arousing as the look in his darkly mysterious eyes. She knew exactly what was going to happen, but could not stop herself waiting for it.

Slowly, silently, Lysander reached out to her. She was unresisting, so he drew her into his arms for a kiss that made her forget everything—until she remembered that she was in the grip of a serial womaniser. With a heart-rending effort she forced herself out of his grasp.

'Lysander! You promised you were going to take me to my door and no further!'

He pointed towards the floor. Without knowing what she was doing, Alyssa had stepped over the threshold. She was now out in the hall again.

Lysander was already coolly backing away from her. 'I was as good as my word. That is exactly what I did. No more—but no less, either.'

With that, he blew her a kiss, turned and sauntered off.

Alyssa was rooted to the spot. She watched him go,

her fingertips resting on her lips as she tried to recapture the pressure of his mouth against hers. When he reached the top of the stairs, he stopped and glanced back. His smile told her everything she didn't want to know. It took her right back to those few delicious seconds she had spent in his arms. She responded with a sudden rush of sensual warmth. Her body would have done anything to experience his strength surrounding her again.

But her heart was too afraid…

CHAPTER THREE

EARLY next morning, Lysander appeared in the nursery doorway. His unexpected arrival threw Alyssa into a panic, but she was careful not to show it. She was briefing her members of staff when she saw him, and didn't want to betray her feelings in front of them. Luckily, this wasn't a social call. He stayed brisk and business-like as he informed them he was arranging for the royal household to fly back to Rosara in a few days' time.

'Once we get there, instead of Ra'id taking tea in my suite I thought we could take him out for a picnic every afternoon, Alyssa,' he told her.

She nodded, glad he was keeping things light and impersonal. 'If the weather's good, it'll be a great idea.'

'Don't worry about the weather, it's the company that matters,' he said teasingly, then walked off, with nothing more than a wink for the other girls.

Alyssa went back to her work in a haze of regret. She might have had more sense than to be seduced by Lysander last night, but it was a near thing. His touch had ignited a slow burning fire inside her that couldn't be extinguished. She knew she should have kept right out of his grasp. All she could do now was try and feel glad that at least she'd found the strength from

somewhere to push him away. If she had given in to
the temptation, let him go all the way and seduce her,
how much worse would she be feeling this morning?
She would be tortured by regret as well as feelings of
loss. As it was, she felt as though a sticking plaster had
been wrenched off her heart—the heart that her ex-
fiancée had broken and Lysander now endangered once
again, just as she was trying to heal. She was so afraid
the edges of her mental wounds were coming apart
again, too. If that happened, there would be nothing
to hold back the flood of her bad memories. And then
all those mistakes would return to haunt her.

Over the next few days, Alyssa barely saw Lysander.
He was too busy arranging their transfer to Rosara to
spend more than a few minutes with Ra'id each day,
over tea. At those times Alyssa kept out of the way,
using the excuse that she wanted them to get to know
each other without any distractions. That didn't stop
her keeping a discreet eye on Lysander from the next
room. She told herself she was only being professional,
but that wasn't true. The way he smiled each time she
opened the door to him made her blush so furiously
she could barely meet his gaze.

The rest of the time, all she got was a glimpse of him
in passing now and again as she and Ra'id settled into
their new routine, or she heard the sound of his clear,
calm voice ringing through the house. Those tantalising
hints of what might have been made him all the more
desirable. All Alyssa could do was go on telling herself
she had been right to push him away, and try to keep
her mind off him. It was almost impossible, but packing

all Ra'id's things ready for the journey to Rosara gave her hardly any time to brood. She already adored the little boy. Getting him to tell her all about his home far away strengthened their bond and cheered him up, too. While he painted pictures of his ponies and spun stories about life in Rosara's Rose Palace, Alyssa told herself life couldn't possibly get any better.

If only she could stop thinking about Lysander. And if only international travel didn't involve flying...

On the night before they were due to leave for Rosara, Alyssa sat up late. She pretended she was collecting things to keep Ra'id occupied during the flight, but the idea of sitting in a tin can hurtling through the air thousands of feet above the ground had a lot to do with her sleeplessness. Only in the early hours of the morning did she finally give in and go to bed. She had barely closed her eyes when the alarm buzzed in her ears.

Ra'id was so excited about going back home he was a real handful, but Alyssa was determined he should behave. They ate a quiet breakfast together in the nursery wing, though she barely had an appetite. Then she marched him downstairs to the entrance hall. Lysander was already there, supervising the transfer and as smartly dressed as ever.

The moment he spotted her, he strolled over to meet them at the bottom of the stairs. Ra'id was delighted, but Lysander was more interested in Alyssa.

'What's the matter?'

'Nothing, Lysander.'

'I hope you are being a good boy?' he warned his nephew.

The little boy blinked up at them both innocently.

'He's fine,' Alyssa said quickly. 'We're getting used to each other, gradually.'

'But there's definitely *something* different about you.' Lysander's hand went out to her, but he brought it sharply back to his side before it went anywhere. 'If you're still worried about what happened on your first night here—' he murmured.

If they had been alone, Alyssa knew he would have reached out to her, which could so easily have turned into something more. The urgent need to feel his touch again filled her until she couldn't speak. All she could do was shake her head.

That wasn't enough for Lysander. 'So what *is* your problem?'

'What problem?'

He gave up. 'OK. I'm taking the lead car for the drive to the airport while you and Ra'id follow in the one behind, so I'll speak to you again once we're on the plane.' Lysander rapped out the words like a warning.

Alyssa felt herself going green. Luckily, Lysander didn't notice. He was distracted by a furious wail from Ra'id.

'No! I want to go with you, Uncle Ly!'

Alyssa frowned. 'You can at least ask properly, Ra'id. Now, we've been working on this. What should you have said?'

The little boy gazed at her for a few seconds, and then remembered.

'Please, Alyssa, may I go in Uncle Ly's car?'

She smiled gravely. 'Well done, Ra'id, although it all depends on your uncle. Your Royal Highness?'

She looked up at Lysander, expecting only an answer to her question. She got a whole lot more. He was gazing down at her so intensely that, for a moment, every one of her fears vanished.

'I think that would be a very good idea, Alyssa.'

She stood up again and bowed slightly. 'Then I'll arrange to have Prince Ra'id's things moved into your car.'

'There's no need for that. I'll ride with you in your car, instead.'

Alyssa felt her face relax in a smile of relief.

'That's better,' he murmured to her as they all moved towards the front door. Alyssa thought she felt a slight touch on her arm, but when she looked down there was no trace of his hand. It didn't matter. Knowing Lysander would be sitting in the same car with them was a welcome distraction. It would give her something other than the flight to think about on their drive to the airport.

As they got to the great front door of Combe House Ra'id broke away and frolicked out into the sunlight.

'I want to sit next to the driver!'

'I thought you might!' Lysander laughed, with a quick sideways smile at Alyssa.

Unable to stop herself, she blushed. As they stepped out of the house the dazzle of bright sunlight reflecting off three highly polished limousines made her blink. It was the perfect excuse to look away from Lysander and hide her nerves. As their chauffeur settled Ra'id into the front passenger seat Lysander reached out and opened the rear door for himself. Alyssa couldn't look at him directly, but made the most of the glimpse she got of his lean, golden-tanned hand. Suddenly, he stood aside.

'After you, Alyssa. Since you're trying to teach Ra'id to be a gentleman, I will of course lead by example! For tips on gentlemanly etiquette, you need look no further than me.'

There was a twinkle in his eyes that was downright wicked and it helped defuse the tension she was feeling, Alyssa smiled back at him in spite of herself and slid demurely into the car.

'Now *that's* more like it.' He slid into the seat beside her and slammed the door. Pressing a button, he raised a partition that closed the passenger compartment off from where Ra'id was busy distracting their chauffeur.

The second they had complete privacy, Lysander lost his smile. Turning in his seat, he levelled a penetrating stare at her.

'Joking apart, what *is* the matter, Alyssa? Are you ill? You're as white as a sheet, and you look terrible.'

She managed to rally, but it was an effort. 'Well, thank you very much! I thought you said you were a gentleman?'

Twisting her hands nervously in her lap, she steeled herself to tell him the worst. It had been preying on her mind, and now it felt like the most awful, enormous problem in the whole world.

'You're right. I am worried about something.'

'Well?' He narrowed his eyes. 'Don't tell me you're having second thoughts? Watching you with Ra'id, it's obvious you're made for each other.'

She felt a wonderful rush of pleasure that made up for all her nervousness about travelling with him.

'Thank you! Looking after him doesn't feel like work to me. I love it so much, and everyone here is so friendly. I can't believe I nearly missed the chance to work for you, Lysander. It's turning out to be a dream job for me,' she said, but he wasn't taken in.

'So what has stolen the roses from your cheeks?' He raised one finger and started to trail it down the side of her face. Alyssa started. Her eyes flicked to where Ra'id and the chauffeur were deep in conversation, just the other side of the soundproof screen. Lysander raised an eyebrow, but dropped his hand. 'Not me, that's for sure. I can see by that blush.'

'I keep telling you, Lysander, it's nothing you need to worry about,' she said in a dangerous voice.

He raised a sardonic eyebrow. 'Well, have it your own way—but remember, if there's ever anything I can do to help, just ask.'

'Thank you. That's very kind,' she said as he offered her a drink from the car's chiller. Pouring some freshly squeezed passion-fruit juice into a glass filled with ice, he handed it to her with a shrug.

'One of the perks of "working for a prince", that's all,' he said with a devastating smile.

When he looked at her like that, Alyssa saw why hordes of beautiful women flocked around him despite his easy-come-easy-go reputation. She also realised her body wasn't as determined as her mind. It melted under the warmth of his gaze, despite what he said next.

'And as Ra'id's nanny, that means you'll be travelling with him and me in the private quarters of the plane, apart from the rest of the staff. You should be quite comfortable as there is a lounge area aside from my office. While there are some matters I must attend to I want to reassure you that I intend to look after my nephew properly.'

'Of course. That means we'll all be able to get some work done,' she said, trying to sound firm.

Lysander's smile became more of a rueful grimace as he nodded towards Ra'id's small, excitable figure in the front seat. 'I wouldn't be so sure about that!'

As usual, Lysander and his team were fast tracked onto the plane so he could start work straight away. He was glad of the excuse to bury himself in paperwork, because he needed time to think. Alyssa was starting to affect him far more than he'd expected. She was stealthily stripping away all his certainties about women. He loved women in all their forms and, so far, wanting a woman and sleeping with her had been one and the same thing to him. He had never met one who didn't want to gratify her desire for his body within minutes of meeting him. Alyssa was no exception, but for some reason she was determined to fight it. Despite her reticence, nothing could hide the signs. He loved watching the pupils of her breathtakingly blue eyes grow large and dark when she looked at him. When the tip of her tongue danced sensuously over her lips it betrayed her thoughts until he wanted to kiss her senseless.

He moved irritably in his seat. Trying to settle himself was impossible, especially as she passed by just then with Ra'id and gave him the briefest of smiles. It wasn't enough. He was hungry for Alyssa's laughter. No other woman looked at him like that, or stood up to him the way she did. It was the effect she had on him that concerned Lysander. Women who wanted money or status were easily dealt with, but Alyssa wasn't like that. She was an unknown quantity. Simply bedding her would pose no problem for him at all. He knew she would come to him, sooner or later. He saw it every day in her eyes, felt it in her touch and, for a few spellbinding seconds, he had tasted it on her lips. Yet each time he tried to get closer, she backed off. It seemed as though life leant too heavily on her mind to let the real Alyssa inside the starchy nanny out to play. That thought ran through his chest like a rapier blade. Lysander knew all about secrets, and the way they could lead to disaster.

He pulled a hand down over his face, blocking out the memories. He didn't want to think about the past in any more detail than that.

And that was why he found Alyssa so disturbing.

Alyssa was not happy. Ra'id's excitement made her feel ten times worse about being so nervous. She made herself join in with him, while fighting to hide her fear. She wished she could be like the rest of the staff, laughing and joking while they stood on the tarmac as they waited to board the plane. When Lysander had jokingly told her, *Cheer up, it might never happen!* she'd snapped at him without meaning to. That made her feel even worse.

Ra'id couldn't wait to be shown to his seat in Lysander's private quarters. Alyssa followed him, glad to be well away from the rest of their party. While a stewardess strapped Ra'id into his seat for the flight, Alyssa sat and shivered. She hardly noticed when

Lysander asked for a blanket, but she was soon very glad he had. Taking the seat beside her, he threw the blanket over her lap and arranged it round her. As the engines rumbled into life he slipped his hand under its folds and caught hold of her hand.

'I was right. You looked cold, and your hand is freezing. Are you sure you're all right, Alyssa?'

He sounded so concerned she shook her head, but couldn't open her eyes. Only the smallest shiver of apprehension betrayed her.

'Oh, is *that* it?'

She heard a mixture of relief and triumph in his voice. Then he gave her hand a quick squeeze and announced loudly, 'Ra'id, Alyssa has a headache, so you must be very quiet.'

Leaning close to her, he whispered very softly in her ear, 'Why didn't you tell me you're afraid of flying?'

'It seemed silly to bother you with something I have to deal with myself.'

'That's a typical Alyssa answer!' He laughed quietly. 'Good. It means you're still there underneath the nerves.'

'Thank you for understanding, Lysander,' she muttered under her breath.

'Don't mention it. Thank *you* for being so brave.'

The royal jet began to thunder down the runway. Lysander held her hand tight until they were airborne.

'There. That's all there is to it,' he reassured her, withdrawing his hand from beneath the blanket. 'Although you still look pretty frail. Why don't you go and have a lie down? I have a bedroom for long haul flights.' He indicated a door behind them. Alyssa was on her guard instantly, and saw him realise why.

'You don't need to worry about me. I'll be far too busy out here, what with paperwork, and Ra'id...you know,' he said casually.

'As kind as your offer is I really shouldn't, Lysander. It's my job to be here to keep an eye on Ra'id, and if you're busy with work—'

'Nonsense,' he interrupted her. 'I will need you to be on top form once we land and return to the palace. Ra'id is bound to be bursting with excitement then and will need some calming down. I'll get another staff member to play some games with him until I am free to entertain him myself. I'm giving you an order to rest.'

Alyssa nodded. After her restless night, the chance to catch up on her sleep and ignore her fears for a while—even if it was in the surroundings of Lysander's own room—was too tempting to miss.

He showed her into a compact cabin. It was perfectly equipped and totally unthreatening, she was glad to find. The carpet was so thick, it felt quite natural to kick off her shoes and dig her toes into its softness as she looked around. The bed was large and uncluttered with the duvet and pillows covered in a plain tan slip. The masculine theme continued through to the room's brown upholstery and the air seemed tinged with the faint suggestion of his signature aftershave.

'Stay in here for as long as you like, Alyssa.'

His guiding hand gave her a light pat.

'Thank you.'

There was nothing forced about her smile now. As she went towards the bed Lysander reached out and pulled back the duvet for her. She hesitated, eyeing him with suspicion. Taking the hint, he dropped the coverlet and took a step back from the bed. With that reassurance, she got in. Before she could stop him Lysander covered her over. It was like being enveloped in a cloud. She closed her eyes. There was a slight pressure from his hands as he settled the cover around her. It eased, returned again for a fraction of a second, and then was gone.

'Try and get some rest.'

His words came from somewhere safely over by the door. Alyssa smiled without opening her eyes. After her long, sleepless night, she really couldn't stay awake any longer.

Lysander didn't leave the room straight away. He paused, then on impulse returned to her bedside the moment she was asleep. After a second's hesitation, he kissed her lightly on her cheek.

'Sweet dreams,' he murmured, and then quickly left the room.

Why in the world did I do that? he wondered, making his escape. He closed the door behind him, but that was the last sensible thing he did. He didn't stride away, putting a good distance between him and temptation. Instead, he stood with one hand on the door handle, thinking.

There was only one problem with Miss Alyssa Dene—and that was the fact that there *was* no problem. She had the body of an angel, and a mind to match.

That was the highest praise Lysander could give. He'd known a lot of women, but they were all too easily distracted by his money and influence. None of them had shown a fraction of Alyssa's nerve and determination. There was no doubting her courage. She didn't think twice about standing up to him, and the way she hid her fear of flying from Ra'id was so brave. When he'd held her in his arms the other night, it had aroused an urgency within his body that was completely foreign to him. And as for kissing her...well, that was something else...

Lysander forced himself to push thoughts like that to the back of his mind. He liked to retain control of his body and emotions at all times. He only had to think about his brother's disastrous love affair to see what happened when a man let his heart rule his head. But Lysander had started leaving his common sense behind whenever he thought of Alyssa. She stirred primitive feelings in him, and they couldn't be ignored. Seeing her looking so vulnerable in his bed, he had been overcome in a shocking way by the urge to possess her fragile beauty.

He was still for so long, Ra'id stopped chewing the end of his crayon and looked up from his colouring book.

'Is Alyssa all right, Uncle Ly?'

'Oh, yes.' He nodded, although his face was grave. 'She's perfect.'

And that's dangerous, he thought.

CHAPTER FOUR

ALYSSA stretched out luxuriantly, still hazy from the dream she'd just had. Opening her eyes, she lurched back to reality. This was Lysander's bed, and she was still in his cabin on-board his private plane. Only the touch of his lips had been a dream. The wonderful, guilty feeling of being held in his arms slipped away as she woke fully, leaving her alone again. It wasn't his pulse she could feel purring through the length of her body, but the soft vibration of aircraft engines.

That was enough to get her moving. She wished she could enjoy Lysander's own private space, but the sensation of being in a plane played on her nerves. She needed distraction, and was about to get up when sounds of soft movement came from outside the bedroom. She froze. Without knowing why, she shut her eyes again and rolled onto her side with her back to the door. There was something about being found awake in this room that felt all wrong, and her only defence was to play possum. Whoever was coming to investigate was bound to let her sleep on. That would be less embarrassing all round.

She heard the cabin door brush over the thick carpet as it was pushed open. She expected her visitor, whoever it was, to retreat after a quick peek. Forcing herself to breathe slowly despite her pounding heartbeat, she waited to hear it close again. It didn't happen. Instead, muffled footsteps crossed the room to her bedside. Despite straining her ears she hardly heard a sound, but there was a definite presence very near to her. She felt it grow closer as someone leaned over her—and she inhaled the clean fresh scent of Lysander's aftershave. It gave her such a lift she let her eyelashes part a fraction. When she saw the pale shape of his hand drifting towards her cheek she drew in a long lingering breath, waiting for his touch.

It never came. His hand hovered beside her face, then moved down to linger over her shoulder. He was almost touching her—but his fingertips never quite connected with her body. The suspense stroked an exquisite glow over her skin. Then she saw his fingers clench. Abruptly, he pulled his hand out of her restricted field of view. Her heart sinking, she waited for him to vanish and quietly close the door on her fantasy.

When he slammed it with enough force to demolish the place, Alyssa didn't have to pretend to jump—she did it naturally. She sat up sharply in the bed, then remembered she should be half asleep. Rubbing her eyes, she pretended to be confused. Lysander was standing in the doorway, looking carefully at everything else in the cabin, but not her. Alyssa was glad she wasn't the focus of his attention. It meant she didn't have to meet his eyes.

'Come on, Goldilocks, it's time to get out of my bed. Alyssa!' he called across the room.

Oh, why couldn't you have thought of Sleeping

Beauty instead? she thought, but deep down she knew. It was the same reason why he hadn't shaken her awake. That would have bridged the invisible dividing line between them—the one she had been so keen to draw. His bedroom was the place where it was stretched so thinly, Alyssa was glad Lysander was the one making sure things didn't get too personal. The reason for her being here in his bed was awkward enough. She already felt at a disadvantage, and wouldn't have known what to say.

'You'll have to get your seat belt on for the landing,' he announced as she checked her watch.

She sighed, but it had nothing to do with sleepiness. It was such a let-down to get up and leave all that comfort behind. Lysander's on-board office was geared up for work, not fantasy. She had experienced a lovely dream, but that was all. He had made waking her up nothing more than a chore, to be ticked off his 'to do' list. Given his casual attitude to women and her damaged feelings, Alyssa knew it was probably just as well. Trying to hide her mixed feelings about that, she busied herself getting Ra'id ready for touchdown. To distract herself, she risked a look out of the nearest window as she fastened his seat belt. If anything could take her mind off Lysander, it was the reminder that she was on a plane.

As the clouds thinned the lion-colored landscape of Rosara became visible below. Alyssa's stomach lurched, and not only through fear. She hadn't anticipated the way she would feel when seeing Lysander's country. His beautiful land appealed to her heart straight away, in the same way something about him reached out to her. It was a mystery, just waiting for her to explore…

The moment they landed Ra'id bounced out of his seat. Alyssa was glad of the excuse to chase after him. She couldn't wait to get off the plane, but Lysander caught her arm as she passed him. She looked back, and her reaction made him let go instantly. He raised his hand in a wordless apology.

'I thought you might like to let me go on ahead, Alyssa. That's all. I'm more used to the reception committee,' he began, but his cabin crew were already swinging the aircraft's door open.

She caught Ra'id's hand before he reached the top of the steps, and she was almost thrown backwards by a wave of noise. Looking out of the plane, she registered the huge crowd of people gathered around Rosara's small airport building. They were lined up around the roof, the balconies and spilling onto the airstrip. Panic almost swamped her. She gripped Ra'id's hand, but the little boy was in his element.

'Wave, Alyssa!' He laughed, but all she wanted to do was dive back into the plane. She half turned, but Lysander was right behind her. There was nowhere to run, but suddenly that didn't matter. She couldn't move. The change in Lysander was so amazing, she wasn't going anywhere. Acknowledging the cheers of his people, he seemed taller and more impressive than ever. Everything that had intrigued her about him was magnified under Rosara's golden sunlight.

Rising to the occasion, he lifted one hand to salute the crowds. They went wild with delight. Lysander must be as popular with his people as he was with supermodels and celebrities! Swept up in the romance of it all, Alyssa couldn't help being impressed. She had wondered if Lysander saved his best behaviour for abroad, making his home ground the place where he was Player King. Instead, he looked every inch the suave, sophisticated statesman. With one hand on Ra'id's shoulder, he encouraged the little boy to wave to their audience. Alyssa decided she might have misjudged Lysander. His country was bringing out the professional best in him. Maybe she would be able to relax her guard a little bit while she was here, after all…

The heat of Rosara flowed over her, filled with exotic sounds and scents. It was exciting, but terrifying at the same time. The breath caught in her throat, and she had to fight the urge to lean back against Lysander's reassuring bulk.

He had no qualms about lowering his head until she could feel the whisper of his words, warm against her neck.

'Are you OK?'

She nodded. 'Just a bit overwhelmed, that's all! Are you always greeted like this when you arrive in Rosara?'

'Pretty much. With so few flights in and out of our country, a royal arrival is always a real event. Practically the entire local population turns out to welcome us home.'

That explains everything, she thought with a rueful smile. *He's playing to the gallery. It's an easy way to impress the maximum number, with the minimum effort.*

Letting Lysander deal with the cheering crowds, she basked in the warmth of his reflected glory. It was lovely to pause, and take in her new surroundings. The atmosphere was rich, and Rosara was well named—The Land of Roses. She could smell flowers with every breath, and it was wonderful. She drank in optimism with the dry air as she walked down the aircraft steps holding Ra'id's hand. With Lysander so close beside her, her dream job was getting better and better.

'There. You've done it. Solid ground beneath your feet at last.' He chuckled quietly.

Alyssa laughed at the sensation of his breath whispering over her hair again. She was glad he had to lean so close to make himself heard over the racket.

'Yes, but you helped me more than you will know, Lysander. Thank you. And it was well worth the journey. I'm so pleased to be here at last. Isn't it terrific? All these people really love you!'

'I know. They always have, but that isn't enough any more, is it?' he murmured with an insight that made her look at him with new eyes. 'From now on, I must earn their respect, too. That's why I must get to work straight away. I should be hustling us straight to the palace.' His grimace told its own story. It was one thing to be the centre of attention, but not so enjoyable when you were in charge of all those individual lives.

Alyssa knew all about pressure. She had been under enough of it herself in the past. But this was on a massive scale.

She thought back to her first sight of Lysander, surrounded by clamouring staff all wanting a piece of him. He had looked as tense as she'd felt then, but arriving home in Rosara had transformed him. He moved today with the ease of someone who didn't have a care in the world. It was only when he mentioned going to the palace that the telltale creases reappeared around his eyes.

'The crowd are enjoying this so much, it's a shame to disappoint them by rushing away. Why don't you send someone on ahead to sort out the most urgent stuff, while you stay here and enjoy your reception for a bit longer?' Alyssa said with a smile. She guessed he might use her words as a good excuse to linger. 'Anyone can see how you've been missed. You and Ra'id really ought to let the crowd get a good look at you both before you disappear behind the black glass of one of your official cars, Lysander!'

The warmth of his presence was quite a distraction in itself, but when his hand dropped lightly onto her shoulder in response to her words, she jumped.

'There's no need for that.'

Lifting his hand again, he pointed across the tarmac. A huge black open-topped limousine was gliding towards them. Surely she wasn't expected to travel in that with him, under the interested gaze of his adoring public?

A chauffeur in full formal uniform and cap opened the car doors for them, saluting as Ra'id bounced into the front seat. Despite his regal status, Lysander stood aside with a smile for Alyssa to get into the rear seat first. She almost died of embarrassment as the crowd greeted this little touch with an extra loud roar of pleasure. From the sound of it, watching Lysander load young women into the back of official cars was a national pastime.

As they drove slowly past the airport terminal a man burst from the ranks of the crowd. The car slowed, giving him time to throw something into the car. It fell into Alyssa's lap. She jumped, then saw it was only one of the famous red roses of Rosara. It was the first of dozens. The car soon filled with flowers, all thrown by the delighted, cheering crowd.

Secure in his popularity, Lysander gave her a lazy smile.

'Wow, I've never experienced anything like this! Your people seem truly happy to have you as Regent.'

Her words had far more effect on him than the jostling press of people around the limousine. He dodged her gaze, leaning forward to reach between the front seats and tousle Ra'id's hair. 'I know. So all I have to do is to build on that. For Ra'id's sake.'

Alyssa wondered if he only tacked on those last few words for her benefit. It was easy to see it was Lysander the people wanted. It was his name they were calling, not the name of his nephew. That made her feel suddenly very uneasy, but she couldn't ask him about it in front of all these crowds. She had to wait until their car turned onto the new main road leading directly from the airport to the palace.

'I need to speak to you, Lysander.' She flicked her eyes meaningfully towards where Ra'id was chatting happily to the chauffeur.

Lysander flipped a switch, and the car's roof slid silently into position. Then he raised the partition separating them from Ra'id and the driver.

'Are you sure it's safe to bring Ra'id to a place like this?'

He gave her a steady look. 'It's his home. You don't need to worry about a thing.'

'Yes, I do. I lost a child because I didn't like making too much fuss, even though I knew in my bones it was the right thing to do. I'm never going to stand by and watch another one suffer. This time I'm going to speak out, whatever the cost to me.'

His looked at her steadily. 'Go on.'

'The people of Rosara are fond of Ra'id because he's small and cute, but most of that love and affection wasn't directed at him. It was meant for you.'

Lysander leaned back in his seat. As their car crossed the trackless wastes of desert he gazed out of the window, running one finger back and forth across his lips. 'Oh. Is that all you're worried about?'

'All?' Alyssa's voice was a squeak of disbelief.

'Let's just say that who the country want as their king isn't uppermost in my mind at the moment. My people want something to celebrate, Alyssa. My— *our*—country was marooned in the Stone Age until only a few decades ago. They don't want that any more. My late father replaced the horrible regime that killed my mother, and started improvements.'

'Your mother was killed?'

His expression shut like a trap. 'Yes. The recent rulers of Rosara don't have a good track record when it comes to wives. My parents were put together by politicians, while my late brother married for love. Both matches led to disaster and death, so I'm saving myself from that. That's why, when it comes to women, I keep moving. Everything I've seen and experienced tells me it's safer that way.'

'I thought men played around for the sake of it.'

Alyssa hid her pain so well, Lysander laughed. 'Yes, there's an element of that. Or at least there was, until my brother died and I was forced to—'

He stopped in mid flow, looked at her and became serious again.

'When I became Ra'id's guardian, and caretaker for my country. That's a job that's every bit as serious as childcare, wouldn't you say?'

'I hope you're not making fun of me.'

This time he recognised that something had touched a raw nerve in her. The half-smile he had been using to try and lighten her mood vanished again. 'Now it's my duty to concentrate on my country, and carry on the good work started by my father and brother. Once I'm up to speed on ruling, I'll teach Ra'id how it's done. Until then, I'm happy to live off my—I mean *our*—people's love until I can earn their respect. If the Rosari are happy, then the Kahani family is happy too. It doesn't matter which one of us gets the credit.'

'I want to believe you,' Alyssa said slowly. 'But when you mention Rosara, sometimes you forget Ra'id. Your instinct is to call this country your own, instead of saying "*our* country" and "*our* people".'

The look Lysander gave her was inscrutable, but he didn't silence her so she carried on.

'You said that your country is in flux. I hope there's no tussle for power going on behind the scenes. It would be terrible for Ra'id if Rosara turned into a war zone.'

Lysander's hawklike glare checked the car's intercom. Their conversation was guaranteed to stay secret, so he relaxed—but only a little. Almost as though he

enjoyed keeping her guessing, he started to smile and
let his expression mature in the heat of her glare. She
refused to back down.

'That won't happen. I do love my country, but I
didn't ask for this responsibility—frankly, I'm far more
comfortable lazing about on yachts. I'll just be thank-
ful when it's over and I can get my freedom back. Until
then, it's my job to keep control of things.'

'Including me?' She narrowed her eyes.

He allowed his soft laughter to caress her. For an
instant she was back in his private cabin, waiting ex-
pectantly beneath his hands.

'I only work wonders, not miracles.'

She lowered her lids in disdain, but his next words
were a teasing throb of promise.

'Don't tempt me to try, Alyssa, or you'll miss your
first sight of *our* palace.'

He spoke in a low, slow combination of notes that
played over her body like fingertips. She turned her
head away. It was one thing for her body to be preoc-
cupied with Lysander, but she wanted to keep her mind
her own. She needed distraction. Glancing out of the
window, she got it.

'What's the matter?' Lysander tensed again at her
gasp.

'I knew somewhere called the Rose Palace had to be
beautiful…but I hadn't realised how big it would be!'
she breathed.

'Do you like it?'

She didn't need to answer. Her amazed silence was
enough.

The Kahani palace had been the home of Lysander's

family for centuries. It stood on the site of the best oasis in that vast, ochre landscape. The afternoon sun was already drawing gossamer shades of apricot and salmon across the sky and sand. Against this exotic colour scheme, Lysander's home stood out like a fairy tale castle spun from sugar. An enormous range of buildings glowed as white as a wedding cake against the tawny desert. Nothing Alyssa had read or seen could have prepared her for this.

It was impossible to believe that such a lovely place could exist in this sea of sand, with its brutal reefs of rock.

As they drew up at the grand south front of the palace Alyssa thought it was the most beautiful thing she had ever seen. Lysander's huge home was built around a vast central courtyard. It had been enlarged and extended over the centuries around the site of the original desert spring, which had been captured in a series of formal pools. Around them, fig and apricot trees cast lots of deep shade. This oasis of calm was overlooked on one side by offices and on the other by a residential wing. Cool, paved corridors and shady courtyard gardens running away from this living heart were the perfect place to spend hot summer days. There were all sorts of places to hide or wander undisturbed. Each large, graceful room inside the palace was more stunning than the next. Delicate traceries of pierced stonework and gold leaf were everywhere. Smiling, bowing servants in flowing traditional dress gave the whole place a fairy-tale feel. It was a completely new world for Alyssa, and she loved it.

Lysander went straight to his office, leaving Alyssa

to be shown around her new home by one of the resident housekeeping team. She was given the pick of several apartments in the nursery wing and chose one overlooking a small, quiet courtyard. Her living room had a little balcony draped with wisteria where she could sit down and relax, when she had a moment to herself. In practice, that might never happen. There were plenty of staff, but in England she had already found she could never rest while Ra'id was up and about. She didn't like to let him out of her sight during the day, and always popped in to check on him during the night, too. Each time she had run her hand over his cool, dry forehead she thought of little Georgie. That had been a rare tragedy, and with Lysander giving her total control over Ra'id's health and welfare she knew the same thing would never happen again, but the worry was always there. She knew everyone else would think she was being irrational, but it didn't feel like that to her. *I'd rather care too much than not enough*, she kept telling herself. *Except when it comes to Lysander...*

Ra'id was so exhausted after all the excitement of their journey home, he wanted to go to bed straight after his supper. Alyssa couldn't believe her luck. Once the nursery was straight, she had a long indulgent bath, got ready for bed, then allowed herself the luxury of a really early night. She was almost as tired as Ra'id, and dropped off to sleep straight away.

Alyssa had been told the nursery wing was fitted with the best alarm system money could buy, but nothing could override her years of training. Her ears were tuned to hear the slightest night-time noise. When music wafted in through her open windows, she was awake instantly. The faint, distant sound of wheels on tarmac told her exactly what was going on. Lysander was having a party. A big affair, judging by the number of vehicles arriving.

She tried to get back to sleep rather than worry about what might be going on, or how much noise there would be. From the sound of it, the party was a long way away. It must be on the other side of the palace complex. Although there was no way a nanny could have expected an invitation to one of Lysander's parties, a part of her couldn't help wishing she were there—while knowing it would be a bad idea. She had seen enough photographs of Lysander partying to know what would be going on. Half-naked starlets would be draping themselves all over the place, hoping for something more permanent than a simple photo opportunity. The more she thought about some other woman making a fool of herself over a philanderer like Lysander Kahani, the harder it was to get to sleep. In the end, she pulled the sheet over her head and stuck her fingers in her ears to block out the distant rise and fall of sound.

A loud knocking at the door to her suite was harder to ignore. Scrambling out of bed and padding over to open it, she found a footman outside. He was carrying a silver salver, and on it was a single sheet of handmade paper. It had been folded in half to hide the message. When she opened it out, she found a simple message written in a bold, flowing hand.

'Dear Alyssa, please bring Ra'id straight down to

the state banqueting hall. I'd like to introduce him to the company.'

It was signed simply 'L', with a little 'x' beside the initial letter.

Alyssa felt the unwanted stirrings of arousal within her body. A personal invitation from Lysander to visit his party, and with a kiss after his initial...

She pursed her lips. It was a dream that, professionally, she had to treat as a nightmare. He was asking her to treat his nephew like some performing animal on display!

She checked her watch, which only made things worse. It was ten past ten—hours after Ra'id's bedtime. Infuriated, she told the footman there was no reply and sent him back to the party. When he had gone, she realised a simple message would never stop a man like Lysander. He would carry on sending for her until she did as he commanded.

Fingering the mobile nursery alarm hanging from its loop at her waist, she wondered what to do. Ra'id was fine—she had checked on him the moment the party woke her, only few minutes before. The security system was switched on, and there was no one else around. She hesitated between taking a chance, and doing nothing in case Lysander took 'no' for an answer. Assuming that wasn't very likely, she decided to take direct action. She would head towards the noise of the party, and give the first member of staff she saw another message for their prince. This time she would send a proper explanation. Slipping his letter into the pocket of her dressing gown, she marched off through the shadowy palace. *I'm not going to wake Ra'id so he can be paraded in front of Lysander's feckless friends as some sort of novelty act!* she thought angrily.

Her plan to pass on a better message didn't work. She didn't meet anyone who could relay it. All the corridors were deserted. It was only when she reached a landing above the great state banqueting hall that she saw someone. A footman in uniform stood beside a pair of wide open double doors. She hesitated, but when he noticed her and smiled she knew there was no escape. Creeping downstairs, she hoped no one would wander out from the party until she had passed on her message. Despite her dressing gown and slippers, the footman listened gravely as Alyssa tried to explain that Ra'id was asleep and wasn't to be disturbed. As she spoke she caught sight of the glittering party going on beyond the open doors and knew she had made a mistake. It wasn't the celebrity drinking contest she had expected. Expensively dressed, respectable couples were being treated to silver service at a formal banquet. The music came from an orchestra that was playing in an adjoining quadrangle while the diners chatted and laughed. Candlelight and the fragrance of good food made her want to linger, but she couldn't risk anyone inside the room spotting her. Ducking out of sight as soon as she had left her message with the doorman, she made a run for it. Her slippers slowed her down so she had barely reached the first landing when she heard someone thundering up the stairs behind her. They were taking the steps three at a time. Only one person would follow her with such silent intent.

'Lysander!'

He caught her arm before she could escape. 'Why are you running away?'

Flustered, she waved at her towelling robe. 'Isn't it obvious?'

'You should have told Gui to leave the door and come in to fetch me. Then you could have given me the message yourself.'

'I didn't want to disturb you...' She faltered.

Lysander looked so smart, it took her breath away. He was dressed in a formal black suit and a purple sash, which was studded with medals. His finery made the contrast between them all the more painful.

'You mean you didn't want to tear me away from the party where I was having so much fun?' he said wryly, making sure Alyssa saw something behind his eyes. 'But perhaps not quite as much fun as you *thought* I might be having when you stormed down here in your wrap to check up on me?' He grinned.

'I wouldn't dream of doing a thing like that!' she snapped, but his widening smile told her there was no point in denying it.

'Well...maybe you're right,' she said grudgingly. 'I thought you wanted me to parade Ra'id in front of some noisy bunch of famous halfwits.'

'You may have a point.' He cocked his head towards the state banqueting hall. The company might be more sophisticated than she had thought, but the chat and laughter were still pretty loud. 'But my real reason for making that request was to show everyone how well Ra'id is being cared for.'

His pride was obvious. Gazing at him, Alyssa for-got everything except the bond she knew was already beginning to grow between Lysander and his little nephew.

'Why don't you go back and fetch him, Alyssa? I'll take good care of him for you, and it'll only be for a few minutes.' He smiled.

It was supposed to be an irresistible request, but it had the opposite effect on Alyssa. It shook her out of her delicious trance, and back into real life.

'I don't think so. Not at ten o'clock at night. He's only five years old, Lysander. He needs his sleep,' she said defiantly, expecting him to argue.

That was the last thing on his mind. He stood back, shocked.

'I had no idea it was that late! The staff only told me about this reception an hour before it happened, when I asked to have dinner served in my suite. My late brother was so disorganised, bless him, that this household practically runs itself. They have been used to telling their king what to do at the last minute. It meant he never had to worry about making any arrangements for himself. It was safer that way. So when I wanted to offer you dinner this evening to welcome you to Rosara…' his voice took on a softer tone '…it threw everything into confusion, and I lost track of time. Of course you're right—I'll go back and tell everyone they'll have to see what a wonderful job you're doing with Ra'id another day. Maybe he could host his own little party. The staff would love to arrange that.'

'Don't make him grow up too fast,' Alyssa warned.

Lysander nodded. 'That's a good point. I had to when I was young, to make sure the staff didn't push Akil, my brother, too hard. It wasn't fun.' His lips became a thin, serious line. 'You're right—I'll tell the assembly they'll have to meet our little star another time, and leave it at that.'

Alyssa smiled. 'They'll understand. I'm sure many of your guests have children of their own. But you'd better get back to your dinner party. You are the host, after all.'

'Yes…and a lonely business it is too, despite all the racket.' He laughed, without sounding happy. 'It's almost as barren as my old celebrity circuit.'

'But much more useful.' Alyssa glanced back along the way she had come, towards the nursery wing. 'I have to hurry back. Even with this, I still worry about Ra'id.' She tapped the monitor attached to the belt of her robe.

'That's why I never need to worry about him when he's out of my sight, because I have you,' Lysander said with a warmth that was completely different from his usual flirting. 'Thank you, Alyssa.'

Dipping his head, he kissed her, in a brief echo of her wonderful dream. It was only the smallest gesture, but it was enough to send heat powering through Alyssa's veins. Instinctively she reached out her hands, sliding them up his arms. It was all the encouragement he needed. His light touch became an all consuming embrace as he crushed her tightly against his body.

CHAPTER FIVE

BEING kissed by Lysander was so much better than any dream. Alyssa relaxed into him as desire welled up within her, blotting out everything but the need to be held and appreciated. It felt so right, she knew it couldn't be wrong—not while it was happening. There would be plenty of time to worry later...

As she softened beneath his hands Lysander's kiss became fiercely possessive. His hand slid to her bottom, kneading it until the fabric of her robe reefed up and he made contact with her warm, yielding skin.

It was a defining moment. As he released her mouth to kiss the gentle curve of her neck she gasped and braced her hands against his shoulders.

'Lysander, no...'

He stopped. Leaning back, he looked at her. His eyes glittered with the need to make her his own and his breathing was ragged. It was the first time any man had looked at her with such naked desire, and Alyssa was spellbound. She knew she should break free and run to save her sanity, but she needed to enjoy her moment, and bask in the sun of his appreciation. For long, spectacular seconds she revelled in the warmth of his arms holding her close and would have done anything to make time stand still. Then he closed his eyes, and with a moan of animal intensity peeled his body away from hers.

Her heart sank as he stepped back. Lysander showed every sign of being equally disappointed. He tried to leave, but couldn't.

'You're right, of course, but...' As he leant forward to place another lingering kiss at the base of her throat his hands flowed over her again for an instant. Alyssa felt her breath catch in anticipation, but it wasn't to be. After another mind-blowing kiss he released her with a long, heartfelt sigh of regret.

'I must go. There are people waiting for me downstairs. This isn't the kind of good example they want.' He breathed, his warmth rippling over the softness of her skin and down into the shadowy depths of her cleavage.

'Yes...' Her body shuddered with a wave of disappointment. Knowing that Lysander wanted her, *really* wanted her, transformed Alyssa. The delicious feeling of power that filled her was like nothing she had known before. She wanted to enjoy all these unfamiliar sensations for as long as she could. A man craved her body and she wanted him in return, with every fibre of her being. Some ancient wisdom told her that, with one word, Lysander could be hers. She could bewitch him into a place where he would forget about his guests, his duties and his responsibilities—but this was Lysander Kahani, notorious playboy. He was a man who must look at every woman like this. A seed of disappointment germinated and grew inside her, feeding on the remains of her common sense. Yes, this was Lysander, lover of all the most glamorous and desirable celebrity women. Being seduced by him would put her in stellar company, and it would mean the world to her. But…

Seducing her would ultimately mean nothing to him. She would be nothing more than another conquest, a number not a name.

Slowly, regretfully, she detached herself from his embrace. If a dull, respectable man like her ex-fiancé could talk of love yet still leave her high and dry, what chance would she have with a rogue like Lysander? His casual approach to women was a warning she couldn't afford to ignore—but his touch was like a drug, making her hungry for more.

Catching at her hands, he drew them up to his mouth. Pressing his lips hard against her knuckles, he kissed them and she felt dizzy with longing.

'Lysander!' she whispered but he had already let her go. His easy stride quickly took him out of her reach. She was rooted to the spot, and could only watch him head off downstairs to rejoin his reception.

When he reached the open doors of the state banqueting room, he turned. Alyssa held her breath, waiting to see if he would look up to see if she was still watching. He did. There was obvious enjoyment in his knowing gaze as he glanced back at her, over his shoulder. Then he blew her a kiss and was gone.

She was left staring after him, her body alive with arousal and her mind full of regrets. Why had she let things go so far? *Because it felt unbelievably good,* a treacherous inner voice told her from its hiding place, deep within her body.

She tried to see sense. Letting Lysander get to her like that left her wide open to more pain. She knew she should have stayed strong, given him the message, then turned her back on him and walked away. Instead she had let herself taste the luxury of being desired by Lysander. Now she knew one kiss from him would never be enough. He inspired a heat within her body that needed to be fed constantly. Reliving the sensation of Lysander's broad back beneath her wandering hands, she wanted to make it reality again. Her mind was so full of him, she had forgotten she was standing in full view of the footman standing at the banqueting hall door. When she accidentally caught the man's eye, fear jolted her back to life. What had she done? Kissing her boss in full view of a witness was bad enough, but when that boss was also a man with no conscience and a country to run, it could mean nothing but trouble. Hot with embarrassment, she turned tail and dashed back to the safety of the nursery wing.

Diving inside her suite, she slammed the door and leaned back heavily against it. Her heart was beating hard and fast, but as it slowed she remembered something. The foootman hadn't looked at all shocked by Lysander's antics. She might as well not have bothered to run. Common sense should have told her that the palace staff must see that same scene, or one very like it, acted out all the time. With Lysander, it would be a new girl every night.

The thought that an escapade that meant so much to her was nothing unusual for Lysander should have made Alyssa feel better.

Instead, it made her feel a whole lot worse. She had

made a fool of herself over Lysander, and she wasn't the only girl to have done that.

But I'm going to be the only one who learns from her mistake, she vowed grimly.

Lysander strode through the huge banqueting hall towards his seat of honour at the top table. The place was packed, and for the first time since he had been forced into the role of Regent of Rosara his smile was genuine. When it came to women, he had always bedded the ones he wanted, whenever he wanted them. He might hate the loss of his free time as his carefree life was replaced by timetables and obligations, but there were advantages. Just when he'd thought he would go insane with frustration, Alyssa had arrived. Right now he didn't miss being out trawling nightclubs or film premieres. He could avoid the noisy press of nightclubs, and the tail of paparazzi that followed his comet of celebrity. His next conquest was close enough to enjoy at his leisure, because she was working right here in the palace. He felt his body kick with anticipation. Perhaps there was something to be said for his new lifestyle after all. In his experience, women only stayed in his life for as long as it took him to get them into bed. For him, the thrill was all in the chase. He needed Alyssa to go on working for him afterwards, so he would have to be careful and very discreet—but that only added to her allure. Breaking down the barriers she had erected around herself would take time, but he would have her sooner or later. There was no doubt about that in his mind. Until then, he would enjoy pushing the boundaries a little more each time they met. It would delay that glorious moment when at last he seduced her, and make it all the sweeter.

His smile widened. He was glad now that he had resisted every instinct to ravish Miss Alyssa Dene at the top of the grand staircase. When he finally satisfied his body and his curiosity about the delights of that delicious, tantalising woman it would be a treat worth waiting for—and he would make sure that everything about the moment was absolutely perfect. Sacrificing his old life of idleness for this new one of routine and duty didn't feel quite such a wrench when he thought about Alyssa. She was not only a delicious prospect, she liked the way he wanted to carry on the improvements to the country started by his father and brother. The idea of making her smile—and not only in the bedroom—appealed to him. It might even turn out to be more rewarding than his old shallow lifestyle on the champagne circuit. Any fool could make a girl go weak at the knees by spending money on her. It took something more to captivate a woman like Alyssa.

Lysander's feeling of satisfaction grew as he saw the way people looked at him tonight. Instead of knowing grins, most of his guests were smiling at him appreciatively. One or two looked as though they would rather be anywhere other than sitting at a formal dinner with a load of stuffed shirts. Lysander knew exactly how they felt. He saved his particularly gracious smiles for them. When they responded with warmth, it gave him a real boost. It was almost as good as the pleasurable feeling he got when he thought about Alyssa.

He had had to walk away from her tonight in favour of this banquet, but his mind wasn't going to let her go so easily. He needed satisfaction, and he couldn't get it from this formal dinner. The only way he could keep smiling at his guests was to think about her. That was ironic. Any of Lysander's entanglements that had threatened to last longer than simple physical pleasure, he had ended. Ruthlessly. It was safer that way. However, while he was still waiting for the right moment to take Alyssa, she was carving herself a place in his thoughts no other woman had managed to secure. Other conquests faded from his mind once he had satisfied his curiosity about them. With Alyssa he got the feeling that the more he found out about her, the less he knew. For instance, that all-covering robe she was wearing. The belt had been cinched in so tightly around her neat little waist it had screamed 'keep away', but he knew that wouldn't have stopped him for long. He let his mind wander in the direction his hands would take at a better time and place...

Their stolen kisses just now had almost taken his breath away. How Alyssa did it he'd never know, but her eager responses to his touch had unleashed his desire in a way that almost had him making his excuses and sidling upstairs to finish what he had started with her, a few minutes earlier. The idea of resisting that temptation was something else that made him smile. In the past he'd have had no hesitation in ditching the formal banquet.

It was exactly the sort of stunt this assembly would expect him to pull. These people were diplomats and politicians who were terrified he would make mistakes. They were all watching and waiting for his first false move. That was why he had been so keen to show off what a good job was being made with Ra'id. He had chosen the best woman for the task, and bringing up the heir to Rosara would be a joint effort. The great and good of his country needed to know its royal family was worthy of their support. *I'm definitely not going to disappoint them on that score,* Lysander thought with determination.

Alyssa barely slept that night. Thoughts of Lysander filled her mind and tormented her body. Her feelings tumbled together in chaos. She had accepted this job convinced that no man was to be trusted, least of all Lysander. That conviction was supposed to make sure she could shrug off his charms. She of all people should have been able to resist! After all the trauma in her life over the past months, she had felt immune to every human emotion. Now she knew that 'numb' was a better word to describe the way she had felt—until she met Lysander. Getting dumped by Jerry only a few weeks before their wedding had wrung out her emotions and she had vowed no man would ever be allowed to disappoint her again. And yet here she was, setting herself up for more heartbreak. Lysander had set her body free to feel again, and he was addictive. She should have walked away every single time he moved in close. Trusting her instincts and keeping him at arm's length might have kept her safe. Instead, she had let him get inside her guard. From that moment, she was as good as lost. She wanted Lysander with a fierce hunger she had never experienced before. It was infuriating and scary and she wanted to turn back time to stop herself being drawn into his web of arousal.

But this torment was so sweet, she wouldn't want to avoid it, even if she could. The only way to protect her heart was to leave this job, and that was something she could never do. The thought that Ra'id would be allowed to run wild again if she weren't there to protect him sent shivers down her spine. Whatever the personal cost to her, it would be easier to shield him from his uncle's lifestyle than to expect Lysander to change...

She sighed. A one-woman Lysander was the ideal, but it was never going to happen. She knew that, but it couldn't stop her dreaming.

Next morning, Alyssa found it hard to concentrate on anything. What she needed was something to take her mind off Lysander. Every thought she had turned to him, and how she could get to see him again. It was the worst thing she could do, but in some mad way she hoped it might frighten some sense into her confusion of feelings. If Lysander guessed how she felt, he would enjoy it so much he might try to seduce her again. If he laughed off the whole incident, she would be crushed. Either way, the idea of being a hostage to his reactions made her feel restless and insecure.

Assuming Lysander would be sleeping late after the banquet, she thought it would be safe to go for a walk. The day was already hot so she got Ra'id to take her on another guided tour of the whole palace while it was still early. It was quite a distraction. Walking through room after room of cool marble floors, silken cushions and gilding was heavenly. The whole palace was magical, but Alyssa couldn't help feeling it lacked something. There was beauty, but no life around. The place was trying too hard to be restrained and tasteful. Ra'id picked up on the lack of atmosphere, too. He was strangely quiet and well behaved.

'That's where all the offices are,' he told her as they ended their tour back on the ground floor. He was pointing along a colonnade that ran down the far side of the main quadrangle. Alyssa wondered if that was where Lysander would spend his days, when he was working. She remembered what he had said about being a caged tiger. This was a sumptuous palace, but for a man like him an office must feel like a prison cell. She looked along the airy corridor for any signs of life, but it was all peaceful.

'Aren't you going to show me inside all those rooms?' she asked Ra'id.

He gasped as though she had suggested putting his head into a lion's mouth. 'Oh, no, I'm not allowed down *there*! But I'll show you how I get the people inside to come out and play with me, if you like,' the little boy went on innocently.

Grabbing her hand, he pulled her out into the court-yard. It was a shock. The heat hit her with as much force as her embarrassment. It was only hours since Lysander had kissed her, and trespassing so close to the place where he lived his other life made her feel strangely shy.

Ra'id led her towards a pool of shade beneath a spreading fig tree. That was when she heard Lysander's voice. He was speaking in a stern, clipped way she had never heard him use before. She stopped, but Ra'id couldn't have cared less about her feelings. All he wanted to do was check out the tree for ripe figs.

As they drew level with an open office door Alyssa saw why Lysander's voice sounded so unusual. Lounging back in an executive chair, he had his feet on his desk and was talking into a small dictating machine. With a smile he raised one hand at them in greeting.

Feeling really self-concious, Alyssa stepped back. Ra'id gave a cheerful wave to his uncle and then turned his attention back to searching for figs. Skulking in the shade, Alyssa tried to become invisible. Lysander had other ideas. He stood up and strolled out of his office to lean on the low wall of the colonnade.

'Alyssa? Don't hide away in the shadows.'

Through the long, sleepless hours of night she had wondered if her memory was playing tricks. Her fantasy Lysander was so handsome and irresistible, she was half afraid the real thing might be a let-down. He wasn't. He looked every bit as good as she remembered. When he looked at her she felt her knees go weak, but that was only the start. His smile seduced her straight into saying too much.

'I have to hide. It's this horrible navy-blue uniform.' She flicked at the stiff skirt. 'I'm not accustomed to wearing a uniform but your staff seemed to think it is the done thing. I look like a relic from the fifties, and feel like I'm wearing a tent. And I'm sorry about last night,' she finished in a rush.

He leaned forward, over the low wall between them. 'I'm not...' he said as he gave her a whimsical grin '...but as for your clothes—if you don't like them, then that's easily fixed. It would be my pleasure to get something done about them.' He smiled at her in a way that explained exactly what his ideas would involve. If that wasn't temptation enough, he was looking spectacular today, despite his late night. Beautifully dressed in a lightweight linen suit, he had slung its jacket over the back of his chair. His usual gold cufflinks were missing and he had turned back the cuffs of his white shirt. They made a dazzling contrast to his bronzed skin.

'So, Alyssa—how are you getting on in your new home, apart from that?'

'Really well, thank you.' She smiled, trying not to enjoy the sensation of his gaze.

'Has Ra'id been showing you around?'

'Yes. I've seen some wonderful things.' *But your smile is the most natural yet,* she decided.

Gazing at him now brought back every stolen moment of the previous night. She could almost feel his kisses again, and so vividly the breath caught in her throat. She blushed.

'Remember what I said before we left England, Alyssa? We can take Ra'id out for a picnic this afternoon, instead of taking tea in the palace.'

She bit her lip. 'I don't know. It sounds perfect, but...' Although she was torn between work and desire, there was never any doubt about what she would say. That didn't make her inner struggle any easier. She tried to put her thoughts into words without embarrassing herself further.

'My first loyalty will always be towards Ra'id. I can't let anything distract me from his care.'

Lysander was watching her carefully.

'Of course. I understand, and I wouldn't expect you to say anything else. It's your work, exactly as showing Ra'id how to behave in public is mine,' he said in a voice so rich with meaning Alyssa had to look away. She couldn't meet his eyes. They filled her mind until she knew she had to escape. Glancing past him, she saw huge piles of paperwork and document boxes neatly stacked on his desk.

'Y-you're busy. We mustn't disturb you any longer.' She drew back, transferring her attention to the little boy. 'Come on, Ra'id—I want to see your ponies.'

'Do you ride, Alyssa?' Lysander asked suddenly. The question was so unexpected, she reacted by instinct.

'Oh, yes, but not for a long time.'

He pounced on the wistful note in her voice. 'You miss it.'

She smiled, remembering her schooldays. 'Actually yes, I do—but I didn't realise how much, until you said that!'

'Then you're in for a treat! When's your next day off?'

'Tomorrow.' She brightened, hoping he was going to tell her members of staff could ride horses from the royal stables whenever they liked.

'Then I'll make a gap in my schedule, and take you sightseeing.'

Her heart soared like a helium balloon until common sense punctured it. 'No. No, I couldn't possibly…'

'We could take Ra'id with us, as chaperone. I want to learn more about Ra'id, so it will be a chance for me to get some experience in looking after him.' Lysander's smile was innocent, but his eyes held wicked temptation.

Alyssa poked some stray strands of hair back behind their grips as she tried to give herself time to think. It would be perfect—a day out with Lysander, no strings attached. All she would have to do was keep Ra'id's best interests at heart, and that was easy enough!

'We'll order a picnic, and you'll have plenty of time to drink in the atmosphere and surroundings.' Lysander's expression was as still as a woodland pool, and equally full of promise. Time with him could lead to only one thing. Gazing deep into his eyes, Alyssa knew he was thinking exactly the same and knew that a whole day in such close proximity would be too dangerous.

'It would be wonderful, but it can't happen, Your Royal Highness. We can go out this afternoon for a short picnic at tea time as we arranged, instead. Maybe you and Ra'id could go on your own instead? You've already told me your country is everything to you. I can't expect such a busy man to find the time to take me out and about,' she said, hoping to emphasise the gulf between them again. She wanted to sound determined, but the words didn't come out like that. Instead, they were full of wistful longing.

'Stranger things have happened.'

His formal smile glittered so irresistibly, Alyssa knew she had to make a stand.

'But not many,' she told him firmly.

Lysander leaned over the low wall, watching them go. Thinking about Alyssa had got him through that tedious banquet the night before. Now it threatened to disrupt the rest of this working day. When she'd mentioned horses, his mind had instantly filled with the idea of racing across the desert sand with her. That was a first. Until now, distraction of any sort always annoyed him when he was dealing with paperwork. For once, the combination of a real flesh-and-blood woman and one of his favourite fantasies was irresistible. He was stirred by the memory of her body wrapped in that soft, ridiculous dressing gown while the expression in her eyes had conveyed that she wanted him so powerfully. It was too much. Lysander started planning for the day when he would eventually sample all the delights she had to offer.

One day, he would spirit her off alone to see The Queen's Retreat.

It was a breathtaking place, and the perfect setting for seduction. Bed was Lysander's cure for every relationship and it had never been known to fail. Unlikely though it seemed to him just now, Alyssa's body would lose its novelty value once he had slept with her. Her mind showed signs of surprising him for as long as he lived, so he didn't have the patience to wait until she bored him. In contrast, sex with her would satisfy his body and stop it hankering after her, once and for all.

He went back to work, and smiled all the way through three drafts of a balance-of-payments statement.

Alyssa wasn't looking forward to their picnic tea that afternoon. She assumed a caravan of staff would turn it into a state visit to the desert, rather than a simple meal in the fresh air. When Lysander arrived alone to collect her and Ra'id from the nursery wing, it amazed her. Flustered, she wasn't quite sure how to react so she kept quiet and let Lysander do the talking.

'It will be just me and my nephew today,' he told her

and the other nursery staff. 'Alyssa is coming along to see fair play, that's all.'

He sounded affable, and his audience looked convinced. That didn't stop Alyssa feeling uncomfortable. She could barely look at him as they walked out to the palace's garage complex. While the kitchen staff loaded picnic things into a brand-new four-by-four, she couldn't stand the suspense any longer. Making sure she and Lysander were out of earshot of everybody else, she tried to broach the subject.

'Lysander, about last night…'

He smiled, and once again Alyssa's body betrayed her. She felt her heart accelerate, and her mouth was suddenly so dry she could hardly speak.

'I should never have let you kiss me—and so you mustn't think you can…' Unable to say anything more, she flicked a glance towards Ra'id, who was bouncing up and down in one of the rear seats of the vehicle.

'Of course I'm not going to try and carry on where I left off. Not today…' He filled in for her, but left his meaning hanging in the air. 'You're at work, looking after my nephew, so I shall be on my best behaviour.' He laid one hand gravely over his heart and dipped his head in mockery of a formal bow. She watched him carefully as he opened the front passenger door for her. It was high off the ground, but when he reached out to help her up there was nothing remotely suggestive about his touch. Alyssa's relief was tinged with disappointment. She wanted him to go further, but told herself this was the only way—especially when he tried to own her with his eyes, as he was doing right now. Her heart had already been broken by a supposedly decent man. This man was a rogue. She'd do well to remember that!

He slid into the driving seat and they started off, out into the desert. At first Alyssa was tense and watchful but Lysander didn't seem to notice. He was far too busy talking to Ra'id.

'I like picnics! I like picnics!' the little boy chanted, bouncing up and down in his seat. He was enjoying himself so much, even Alyssa began to think this trip was a good idea. The sky was blue, they had enough food to feed an army and Lysander really was making an effort to get to know Ra'id.

'I expect you have picnics all the time, living in a lovely place like this,' Alyssa said as they travelled along an ancient dirt road. She was enjoying the sight of hot, starkly beautiful desert sliding past so fast outside, while she was cool and comfortable inside the car.

'No. As far as I know the only time Ra'id went out was to travel between Combe House in England and the Rose Palace.'

'Is that why you suggested this outing?'

He shook his head. 'Having a picnic is something I've wanted to do since I was about the same size as Ra'id.' Lysander smiled, but not at her. With his lips pressed tightly together, he carried on gazing through the windscreen.

'You're not telling me this is the first time you've done this?' Alyssa could hardly believe what she was hearing.

'I've never had the excuse to do it here before. The one dim memory I have of my mother is of her, me, and my brother, Akil. We were in a park in England.

We must have gone out for the day but I can't recall her face, or what she was wearing, what we ate or anything important like that. All I remember is her voice, saying: "I wish we'd done this before. We'll have to do it again some time." But we never did.'

'That's so sad,' Alyssa said softly.

He shot her a strange look. 'The fact that the only real memory I have of my mother is of a time when she was happy?' he queried. 'What's wrong with that?'

CHAPTER SIX

ALYSSA couldn't argue with him. The quiet way he answered her question intrigued her. Was he giving her a glimpse of the man behind his public image? It was so at odds with the passionate seducer who had held her in his arms the night before. When he looked at her now, there was hardly any flirtation in Lysander's smile. She took that as a good sign, and tried to relax.

Sitting in a prestige car with a handsome prince at the wheel, she felt as though a little bit of royalty might be rubbing off on her. She even had to suppress a childish urge to wave regally out of the window. For once in her life she didn't have to worry about a thing. All she had to do was sit back and enjoy being chauffeured around. It was lovely and so, she had to admit, was Lysander. He was behaving perfectly today, as the ideal role model for Ra'id. Away from his office he was off duty, and so was the usual little crease between his brows. Now and again he even hummed along to the gentle sound of Marcello coming from the on-board CD player. With a sigh, Alyssa lay back in her seat and closed her eyes. The sun was warm against her lids and the filtered air was cool. For the first time in ages, life was offering her more than loneliness. The feeling of

Lysander at one with his car and only inches away from her was incredible.

'I suppose you went on picnics with your parents all the time, Alyssa?'

'Mmm? No…they spent most of the year working abroad, so I was sent off to boarding school. I went home for the holidays, which was about as much exposure to me as they could take.'

'Don't sell yourself short,' he said sharply.

She opened her eyes and looked at him. 'What's the matter? I expected you to laugh when I said that.'

'There's nothing funny about a child who sees themselves as a burden.'

'You're getting too fond of Ra'id for him to think that. I can see it every time you two are together,' Alyssa assured him.

'I wasn't talking about him.'

She smiled. 'Oh, don't worry about me. I've long since stopped bothering about how things are between me and my parents.'

Another look at his face told Alyssa he hadn't been thinking about her situation, either. He was staring grimly out of the windscreen at the road ahead.

'Tell me more about your upbringing,' she probed gently. 'Is the Kahani family large, beyond this branch? I meant to do some online research in my spare time to get background, but I haven't got around to it yet.'

'Don't bother,' he said brusquely, missing a gear change. That made him spit out a word in Rosari that Alyssa was glad she couldn't understand.

'No, and there's no royal family beyond me and Ra'id,' he told her. 'That's the whole problem. My father was a second son, like me. His older brother was King, and a cruel, bitter man. His rule kept Rosara in the Dark Ages. My brother Akil and I were lucky. Our part of the family was never expected to inherit the crown, so we were allowed a lot of freedom. Unfortunately, the death of our mother changed all that.'

Alyssa clucked with sympathy. 'My mother and I have never been close, so I can't imagine how awful it must have been for you to lose yours. It must have been a terrible shock.'

Lysander didn't reply straight away. Alyssa assumed it was because he was driving down a tricky, rock-strewn slope. When he spoke, she found out how wrong she was.

'Yes—and no. She was found guilty of adultery, and, as my unforgiving uncle was on the throne at the time, she was beheaded.'

Surprise catapulted Alyssa forward in her seat. 'Oh, my God!' She clapped her hand over her mouth and glanced over her shoulder at Ra'id. The little boy had calmed down enough to look at a comic, and hadn't noticed. Relieved, she turned to stare at Lysander in horror. 'When was this?'

'A long time ago. Thirty years or more—not long after the picnic I told you about, maybe? The riots that followed killed my uncle and put his brother—my father—on the throne. Father was determined things would change, and so am I. That's why I'm going to continue making improvements here.'

He was staring ahead so grimly now that Alyssa felt she had to say something. 'You're right. The sooner you can secure your country's place in the twenty-first century, the better,' she said. It worked.

'That's why I want to make sure Ra'id has a proper childhood. Akil and I never had much experience of life until we were sent to England to finish our education. Our father was quite forward thinking, but even so we had private tutors to begin with.'

'You must have been lonely.'

Lysander shook his head. 'I always had Akil to think about. He was never very worldly, so I always fought in his corner. That made me self-reliant.'

'Too much of that isn't always a good thing.'

'I don't think my brother would have agreed with you. Once he became King and inherited a band of advisors, they took over. I was surplus to his requirements and didn't have anything to do. Hitting the party circuit was a reaction to that. That was why Akil never liked the way I lived my life. He knew I was capable of so much more.'

Alyssa felt on firmer ground for once. 'Then it's a shame he never found you a job. Hard work suits you. You really looked the part when we saw you in your office.'

'Thank you,' he said, adding lightly. 'It sounds as though you actually meant that.'

'Why shouldn't I?'

Sliding a glance wickedly across at her, he laughed. 'Alyssa, I've been flattered by mistresses of the craft. Believe me.'

They crested a rise in the road, which gave them a spectacular view of the plains below. Lysander parked the four-by-four where it would cast the longest shadow, got out and opened the doors for Alyssa and Ra'id. With a squeal of excitement the little boy bounced out and careered off down the slope at top speed.

'Don't go too far!' Lysander called, but Alyssa laughed.

'He's only got little legs. With nothing but a few sparse bushes in every direction, he can't get lost. He'll be fine,' she reassured him, but kept a careful watch on her little charge all the same.

The atmosphere out in the desert was very different from the comfortable, air-conditioned interior of Lysander's car. It was hot and dry. Now and then a light breeze blew up, ruffling his dark curls and wrapping Alyssa's skirt around her bare legs. She was still wary of him, but her warnings seemed to be having some effect. Lysander's interest in her didn't waver, but he kept his distance. Neither spoke as they strolled along in Ra'id's wake. Alyssa's mind was too full of miserable childhoods and loveless lives, and the last thing she wanted to do was inflict her memories on Lysander. For a while they watched the little boy in companionable silence, but Alyssa's gaze was often distracted by their stunning surroundings. Sunlight had spent a million lifetimes baking the stony countryside into a million shades from caramel to cream, and the overall effect was breathtaking.

'It's such a beautiful place,' Alyssa was moved to say after a while. 'How could anyone prefer the big city to this?'

'A life spent in casinos and nightclubs isn't exactly hell on earth. I'm sure you'd be the first one to remind me of that,' Lysander said with dry humour.

'Do you miss it?'

He smiled, but didn't answer.

'I don't think the newspapers expected you to move back here, Lysander. If they knew how well that dinner went, and the hours of routine office work you put in, I'm sure they'd be amazed,' she said quietly.

'The Western press perhaps, but not the press here in Rosara. They've always understood that I left to avoid being sidelined, and I came back because of loyalty. I love this country, and I won't let anything disturb its peace. That's why I want to take such great care of Ra'id. Some of my countrymen don't believe he should be the next king.'

Alyssa was shocked. 'Lysander! When we were driving from the airport, you told me there was no danger to him here!'

Her first instinct was to call Ra'id straight back into her arms and head for the palace and safety. Lysander stopped her with a few simple words.

'Would it reassure you to know that I'm the one they want as their ruler? That there's a faction who think I should be King, rather than him?'

She stared at him. 'I don't know. It depends what would happen to Ra'id.'

'He's quite safe with me. You've got my word on that.' Lysander's accent thickened with honesty. 'He would stay in your care and be my heir until I had a son of my own. That's why I wanted the best nanny for him from the first. Whatever happens, I will always treat Ra'id with the respect due to my brother's son. Looking after him is my priority.'

'And mine,' Alyssa said firmly.

They had both been watching the little boy as he chased lizards over the hot desert rocks. When she said that, they turned and shared a look.

'Smiling suits you, Lysander.' Alyssa laughed. 'You should do it more often.'

His reply was quick. 'You won't believe this, but I was about to say exactly the same thing to you!'

The palace staff had packed an amazing picnic. There was a feast of things Alyssa usually kept off Ra'id's menu, such as crisps and cake, along with healthy slices of perfectly ripe melons, peaches and bunches of fat grapes. While Alyssa set it all out, Lysander produced a pair of miniature radio-controlled buggies from the back of the four-by-four. That was when Ra'id lost interest in the food—and it was the last she saw of the two men in her life until they got hungry.

It was a long time before Alyssa had a minute to herself. Once she'd put the exhausted Ra'id to bed that night and handed over to her deputy, she could officially call herself off duty for the next thirty-six hours. With a relief she didn't usually feel when faced with a holiday, she retreated to her own suite. Her apartment at the Rose Palace was lovely. It was at least twice the size of her city flat in England, and had large, airy rooms. It was a pleasure to wander around it by the light of scented candles, enjoying all the luxury. Flickering shadows danced over pale painted walls and high ceilings, while the fragrance of lilies drifted in from the courtyard garden below her open windows. Although tired, Alyssa was far too wound up for sleep. Her mind was crowded.

She roamed around hoping it would clear, but all she could think about was Lysander. The bed reminded her of his cabin on the plane, where she had imagined his kiss. Her kitchen was stocked with everything to make her feel at home, but that only brought back the way Lysander had helped her to coffee and snacks at their picnic. And every time she felt her pulse speed up, she thought of his kisses…

That moment on the palace landing felt like a lifetime ago. She had seen a side of Lysander today that was at odds with his playboy image. She liked to think her common sense might be having some influence on him, but she couldn't ignore the obvious reason for the change in him. He'd had no time for flirting today. Both he and Alyssa had been too busy taking care of Ra'id and laughing along with him to think of anything beyond their shared interest in the little boy.

She tried to see that as a good thing. Today could so easily be a one-off. Lysander had been taken out of his natural habitat. That might be having the same effect on him as the change in routine did with Ra'id. It gave them both more to think about than mischief. Alyssa tried to see that as a good thing, but the memory of Lysander's eyes burning with desire for her on the night of his banquet was impossible to forget.

She wondered what the next day would bring—more respect, or more temptation? Setting her alarm, she lay down and tried to sleep. The days were long in Rosara, but she was determined to make the most of every second of freedom.

Everything was perfect, right down to the jug of filtered water in her bedside fridge, but she still couldn't switch off. After what felt like hours, she gave up, untangled herself from the sheet and got out of bed. One long, cool, bubbly bath later, smelling of rose petal attar from the royal perfumier, she pulled on a thin cotton blouse and light, summer-weight trousers. Pouring herself a large glass of orange juice fresh from the palace citrus groves, she strolled out onto her balcony. If she couldn't sleep, she could at least suffer insomnia in comfort. Settled on piles of silken cushions specially designed for lounging, she gazed past tendrils of wisteria draped around the balcony rail, and down into the courtyard below.

The night was warm, and heavy with the fragrance of citrus and jasmine. It was heavenly. She stretched her limbs luxuriously across the downy pillows. It felt so good, she needed only one thing to complete the picture. That was a glimpse of Lysander. She hoped their happy afternoon hadn't been a one-off, but she was wary that it might have been designed to weaken her resistance to him. Her body was definitely drawn to his, but she couldn't let that lead her astray. Instead, she fell back on fantasy. Lysander's worldwide reputation as a playboy made him too hot for her to handle in real life, but dreaming was free. She sighed. The man was a twenty-four-carat rogue, and a genuine heartbreaker. You only had to look at him to see that.

She smiled at the thought of his handsome face this afternoon. She had never seen him look so relaxed and happy, especially when he was showing Ra'id how to take pictures with his smartphone. Not even in all those press photographs, where he had a new woman hanging on his arm in every shot.

It was interesting to think he might really change now he was back in Rosara…and it was safer, too. She had heard from other staff at the palace that no woman could expect to keep Lysander interested for long, but maybe that would change, too. As long as he stopped tempting her everything would be fine, although it was impossible not to wonder what it would be like to be on Lysander Kahani's menu…

Alyssa had never met any other man like him, either in looks or character. And whatever his faults, he was always a gentleman. If he wanted, Lysander could have charmed her into his bed at any time over the past few days, if he did but know it! He made her feel so special. *But then,* she thought, *he must have honed his skill at making women feel unique on a thousand other conquests.* A man like that would be an expert at playing games with hearts. Every time she felt tempted, Alyssa relived the mental torture of her breakup with Jerry all over again.

It was supposed to keep her own heart closed to Lysander, but it didn't work. She sympathised with him, and could understand why he was so restless. He needed some form of escape within his gilded cage, she could tell—but she didn't dare try and find out what it was.

Lysander couldn't sleep. He tried paperwork. He went back to his office and shuffled documents, but it was no good. The palace had a complete movie theatre, but trying to watch films only made him feel worse. However hard he tried to distract himself, nothing worked. It couldn't take his mind off the events of that afternoon.

He cursed loudly. What had Alyssa done to him? He couldn't even be truthful with himself any more. It wasn't the picnic that had affected him so much, but *her*. When it came to women, he was a professional. This afternoon he had gone out of his way to act as though their kiss had been no big deal for him. He had tried to pretend it was a mistake he had already forgotten about. That couldn't have been further from the truth. Lysander enjoyed heightening his desire in any way he could. Resisting temptation was a new strategy. It was proving to be the most arousing *and* the most difficult thing he had ever attempted. Alyssa's smile, the scent of rosewater on her warm skin, that little habit she had of twiddling a lock of her hair when she was thinking—details kept coming back to haunt him as night fell. Tiny things about her he hadn't realised he had noticed seethed through his mind until he could hardly think straight. The woman was disrupting his thoughts and stealing his sleep. How was he supposed to work towards a better Rosara, with thoughts of her pressing in on him from all sides?

This had gone far beyond a joke. *No one can be allowed to get inside the mind of Lysander Kahani like this,* he thought with grim determination. He had to put a stop to it as soon as possible, and, being Lysander, he knew exactly how to do it. The sooner she was in his bed, the better.

The palace was winding down for the night. Alyssa got to her feet, knowing she should try to go back to bed. Still she lingered, enjoying the richly fragranced evening air for a few more moments. The sound of a bubbling fountain down in the quadrangle was wonderfully restful. An old apricot tree dripping with fruit scented the air with its sweetness. The evening was so quiet she could hear the soft sounds of the last few servants going off to bed. The rustle of a robe or the click of sandals on marble floors were the only human intrusions into a scene dominated by nature. A warm breeze caressed her skin, insects sang in the shadows and as always there was the scent of the roses that gave Rosara its name.

It was heaven—and then she heard hooves clattering across cobblestones, not very far away. She listened as the sound changed, and knew the royal horses were being led in for the night. Sleep still felt so far away. The stables were close, and she couldn't resist visiting them.

Leaving her rooms, she padded through the silent palace. As she cut through the inner courtyard below her balcony a lighted window on the ground floor caught her eye. She saw a tall and unmistakable form pass a pair of open French doors. It was Lysander. The angle meant she couldn't see his face, but that didn't matter. What she saw was arousing enough. He was pacing around in bare feet, his white shirt hanging loose and unbuttoned. Her heart lurched as she realised he must be in his own suite, on his own territory.

As she was enjoying the sight he suddenly swung out into the courtyard garden. As if sensing the heat of her gaze, he looked straight across to where she stood watching him.

There could be no escape. Alyssa thought of all the photographs she had ever seen of him. None of them did him justice tonight. While he was always snapped with the world's most glamorous women, tonight she was scrubbed clean of make-up, perfumed only with bath oil and dressed in chain-store casuals. She blushed furiously, but before she could melt back into the shadows he spoke.

'Alyssa? What a lovely surprise. I was just thinking about you. You can't sleep either?' He chuckled, his voice as warm as melted chocolate. 'I know how you feel. Our afternoon together was so good, it seems a shame to end this special day like any other.'

He smiled, in a deliciously unthreatening way.

'Wait there—I've had a great idea…'

CHAPTER SEVEN

LYSANDER vanished back into his suite, but reappeared seconds later. Fully dressed now, complete with breeches and boots, he was still buttoning his shirt as he strode across the courtyard towards her.

'I don't need to ask what brings you outside on this beautiful evening, do I, Alyssa?'

'I couldn't sleep, and when I heard the horses I had to go and take a look.'

'Enticing, isn't it?' His voice was full of its old mischief, but that was as far as it went. He stopped while he was still several feet away from her. 'Why don't we go out for a moonlight ride? If you think this palace is beautiful, wait until you see the place they call The Queen's Retreat. It's too beautiful a night to waste an opportunity like this. The gardens there are full of the most stunning plants and flowers, brought from all corners of the world.'

Alyssa stared at him. 'Don't you think it had better wait until morning?'

It was obvious he knew exactly what she meant. A man and a woman in a beautiful garden, caressed by the warm desert night...

He smiled in a way that told her he had already made

up his mind exactly what was going to happen, but he was still careful not to get too close. 'No. It can't wait.'

Alyssa's entire body began to glow. This was her wildest fantasy brought to life. Apart from dim lamps set around the quadrangle, the only lights showing were in his suite. Every other window overlooking the courtyard was dark and blank.

No one would see them leave the palace together. No one would know.

But I will, she thought with a pang, *and so will my poor battered heart.*

'That doesn't sound very sensible…' she ventured.

He shook his head, and spoke in a rich undertone. 'It's possibly the most sensible thing I've done in my life so far.'

Alyssa tried to answer, but couldn't. Desperate to know what he was talking about, she didn't have the confidence to ask. Lysander at arm's length was exciting. Any closer than that, and he was sure to be trouble.

He gave her a little bow and her senses went into overdrive.

'What if someone sees us?'

His dark eyes glittered like jet in the soft evening light. He chuckled softly. 'Little details like that never bother me. When I want to do something, I do it. There's never any point in hesitating. There comes a time when the waiting has to stop—and that's now.'

Alyssa didn't know what to think. Taking a step back, she wrapped her arms around her waist and stared down at the toes of his highly polished riding boots. To look at anything else would lead her into all sorts of trouble.

'I'm not sure...'

'I am—and if we're going at all, it needs to be soon. If we go now we'll be in time to see a full moon rise over the mountain ridge. It's a breathtaking sight,' he murmured, reaching for her hand. 'We should take our chance while we can. It's a perfect night—and we'll use my special short cut.'

Alyssa tried to refuse, but Lysander was impossible to resist. He guided her towards the open French doors of his apartment. She couldn't have complained if she wanted to. Her heart was pounding too hard. She could hardly take it all in—his breathtaking confidence, the faint drift of his aftershave and the enticing glimpses of his private life as she was whisked straight through his suite.

The hall beyond the royal wing was deserted. Lysander melted through the shadows, leading her where he must have led countless other women in the past. They made it to the stables without picking up any of his security team. From there, it was easy. Communicating by the lightest of touches, Lysander helped Alyssa saddle up a beautiful bay mare, and then found his own horse. Together, they escaped into the night.

The royal animals were bred from tough, fast desert bloodlines that Lysander's family had guarded jealously for centuries. Alyssa laughed with delight, but desert breezes stole the sound from her lips. The only sound was the drumming of hooves on hard-packed sand. They galloped across a landscape veiled in the mauve and lavender shades of dusk, to an island of rock in the sea of sand. Cresting a final dune, Alyssa saw the stark silhouette of a royal palace pasted against the clear ultramarine sky.

Lysander led her on, but as they reached the shadow of those great stone ramparts Alyssa reined in her horse. It turned and fretted as she looked up at walls as high and solid as cliffs. Lysander was a little way ahead but when she stopped he wheeled his stallion around and went back to her side.

'Come on—I don't want you to miss a moment!' he called, urging her on past the last security post and up the sloping switchback path that led to the castle gates. As they clattered beneath a final arch, roosting doves exploded with fright across an inner courtyard. Alyssa jumped, but Lysander was there to reassure her.

'There's nothing to be scared of here. It's the safest stronghold in my country. I visit when I want to get away from people,' he confided, which shocked Alyssa.

'But everyone knows you're the original party person!' she blurted out. 'Why would you of all people want to escape?'

'Everyone needs quiet sometimes, and, anyway, I don't have time for partying any more. There's so much to do for Rosara. It fills up all my time, and the change from player to manager is a difficult adjustment.' He leapt from his horse and went to help her down. 'I've always liked my own space. It's especially important to me now. I need a place where I can leave the restrictions of palace life a long way behind.'

Lysander's strong, tanned hands slid around her waist and drew her gently from the saddle. His touch lingered over her for a little longer than protocol would have liked, but here the boring rules of palace life felt far away. For once, Alyssa was in no hurry to remind him about them.

Two men came out from a gatehouse to greet them. One took care of their horses, while the other handed Lysander a flaming torch.

'What a gesture!' Alyssa said, trying not to watch the firelight dance over the impressive, gleaming muscles exposed by Lysander's open-necked shirt.

'It sets the scene perfectly,' he told her. 'There's no electricity here. The Queen's Retreat was the last word in gracious royal living in the fifteenth century, but not now. Queens today want more in the way of hundred-watt lighting, satellite TV and walk-in fridges.'

He held the torch high and looked around with real fondness. Alyssa couldn't help wondering about all his ancestors, living, loving and laughing in this beautiful haven. Inside the perimeter wall was a large courtyard. In the centre rose the castle, but Lysander led her to one side of the main building. As they went he touched his torch to others set up along the way. When they reached a wrought-iron gate set into the stonework, he opened it and let her go through first.

She walked into a beautiful garden, laid out behind the main castle. It was a wonderland of rustling trees and tangled undergrowth, rioting around a large circular building with a high domed roof.

'That's the observatory,' Lysander told her in passing. 'This is the perfect place to study the stars, and I like to relax in style.'

Everywhere was studded with the luminous pale flowers of roses and lilies, sparkling with fireflies that danced in the dark.

Alyssa drew in a deep breath, rich with all the wonderful perfumes of flowers and oil from cedar trees.

Before she could say anything, a nightingale began sobbing from deep in the heart of a rambling rose.

'Legend says that is the lament of an adulterous queen who was banished here,' Lysander said in a low voice.

'Who could be unhappy when they can listen to that?' Alyssa whispered, afraid to spoil the moment. 'Unless she regretted putting her trust in someone who betrayed her?'

'It sounds as though you know what you're talking about,' he whispered back.

'Shh.' Alyssa put her hand on his arm. It was only a touch, but it was enough to make him tense. When she felt that, Alyssa looked at him quickly. Their eyes met, and in the silence a second nightingale sent a stream of silvery notes into the evening. For long moments they waited until the song died away. Then Lysander's hand slid over hers.

'Come on, or we'll miss the real show.' He squeezed her fingers, but then moved away.

Light-headed with the effects of his touch, Alyssa followed. He led her over to the Eastern wall, where a golden glow was already spreading above the horizon. Climbing a steep flight of steps to the sentries' walkway, Alyssa gasped at the perfect view of the night sky it afforded.

'It's lovely and you can see for miles!'

Lysander put out the torch he was carrying, then leaned his folded arms on the breast high wall.

'Yes, but can you imagine spending every day and night here, for the rest of your life?' he said quietly. 'Marooned far away from the city, the bright lights and all your friends?'

'I'd love it,' she added, smiling at the confession he had made.

'I had a feeling you would. It isn't for everyone, and that's part of its charm. My brother Akil wanted to update this place and make his wife move here, but she hated it.'

'I wouldn't have bothered waiting for the renovations. I couldn't have got here fast enough,' Alyssa muttered.

He laughed. 'You're the first woman who hasn't run screaming from the thought of being stuck here at The Queen's Retreat without so much as a power shower to bless herself with.'

'I'm a nanny. We can cope with anything!' Alyssa joined in his laughter.

'Then you're the only woman I've met who could. Most of them have fainted at the thought of a hangnail.'

Alyssa put her elbows on the wall beside him and cupped her chin in her hands. 'Then you've only met some rather silly women! I'm glad I'm not like that.'

'So am I,' he said, then looked away quickly and cleared his throat. 'This place is so beautiful, I'm determined to make it happy, too.'

'It feels wonderful to me already,' Alyssa said dreamily. A light breeze whispered in from the desert, but the castle's ancient stones had been storing up the sun's fierce heat all day. Dusk drew enough warmth from the walls to keep them comfortable, but Lysander was obviously enjoying his role as host.

'Let me know when you've had enough. For myself, I could stay here all night.'

'So could I,' Alyssa sighed. As they watched the

glowing moon rise slowly over the stark line of the distant horizon she shivered with the romance of it all—the nightingales, the flowers and Lysander, all bathed in moonlight.

It was the only encouragement he needed to slide an arm smoothly around her shoulders.

'Let me keep you warm,' he murmured, his voice low with desire.

Without a word Alyssa stepped sideways, just far enough to slip from his grasp.

Lysander paused. Alyssa's refusal to be taken for granted was one of the first things that had appealed to him. Now it was starting to get tired. Women never refused him. It simply didn't happen, but, more than that, he knew Alyssa was longing for his touch. He toyed with the idea of simply walking away without risking his dignity any further, but decided that wasn't an option. If he did that, he knew his memories of Alyssa would haunt him for as long as his life lasted. While there was the smallest chance of softening her bewitching eyes with satisfaction, he knew he would never be free from her.

It was the simplest thing in the world to reach out to her again. This time she flipped his hands away with more determination, even as she quivered with longing.

'Please don't!'

He was getting frustrated with her now; he could sense that she wanted him as much as he wanted her, so what was holding her back?

'Why do you do that, Alyssa?'

'It's nothing personal.'

'Exactly!'

She had been gazing away across the plain, refusing to look at him. When he said that she whipped around. His expression stopped her doing anything as silly as laughing. He was tight-lipped with arrogance; humour was the last thing on his mind tonight.

'You are *unbelievable*, Lysander Kahani!' Her eyes flashed.

'You make it sound like a character reference.'

'Then congratulations. I'm sure you're delighted.'

'Of course I'm not! This is ridiculous,' Lysander countered. '*You* are ridiculous. How can my touch possibly make you so unhappy? Good God, woman—why the hell did our paths have to cross? Why couldn't you have settled down with a nice, respectable middle-class man in an English suburb and raised a flock of nice, respectable middle-class children before I ever set eyes on you?'

Alyssa shuddered. 'No, thanks. I've been there, and done most of it.'

'And what is that supposed to mean?'

She dug her elbows into the weather-worn stones of the wall and dropped her chin onto her hands again. 'I'm not telling you. Why should I tear myself up about it all over again, when you've just told me you wish we'd never met?'

'I never said that!'

'Why should I torment myself by raking over my past when you'll only tell me not to be so stupid and that I should pull myself together and get on with my life?'

Her words instantly made him suspicious. 'That's not the Alyssa I know speaking! Why put someone else's words into my mouth? I...' he said, straining his frustration through clenched teeth, 'I...would *never* say that to you.'

'Huh.'

She went on staring fixedly into the distance.

Lysander could only see her in profile, but he knew the defiant glitter in her eyes had nothing to do with the reflection of the moonlight. He fought the impulse to pull her together himself, and none too gently. Instead, by taking several deep, considered breaths he managed to summon up a scrap of tact.

'You're cold, Alyssa,' he growled. 'Come into the observatory. A full moon isn't ideal for stargazing, and supper will be waiting for us.'

Pivoting on his heel, he stalked off to the circular building in the heart of the garden. Sliding back a panel in its wall, he revealed a huge telescope trained on the night sky. Then he turned to call her closer and was shocked to find she had already done as he said. She stood a few feet away, watching him guardedly.

'Come in, and tell me all about it.'

He was making an effort, and wondered how far he could carry it. From her expression, Alyssa was curious about that, too. Without a word, she followed him into the observatory. It was as richly furnished as the Rose Palace, and tonight its central table had been hurriedly set with a delicious buffet and armfuls of fresh flowers. Lysander opened a bottle of champagne, poured a glass and held it out to her.

'So you've been married, Alyssa?'

She shook her head. 'No. I—I was engaged to a guy called Jerry, but that ended months ago. He was married to his job, but then so was I. It worked when things were going well, but then…'

She faltered. At that moment the nightingale's song swelled up with such power, it seemed to inspire her. She accepted the glass from him, and took a quick sip. Then her chin went up and she looked him straight in the eyes.

'I've got nothing to be guilty or ashamed about. I did nothing wrong—he was the one who had an affair.'

'Some men do that,' Lysander said, though he'd always been careful to make sure one dalliance was over before the next one began.

She looked out towards the rose thicket where the nightingale carolled on. 'I know that now, so next time I shall be ready—' She began strongly enough, but couldn't carry on. Suddenly words failed her in a cry of pain.

This wasn't part of Lysander's game plan at all. Alyssa was supposed to throw herself into his arms, not dissolve. There was only one thing to be done, so he did it. He grabbed hold of her, pressed her head against his chest and let her cry.

'But there will be a next time,' he reassured her softly. 'You know that, don't you?'

She nodded, and that was his cue to hold her tighter still.

Alyssa was lost. She cried and cried until she was too exhausted to do anything but let her last few tears trickle away. Only her ragged gasps went on, bouncing her face against the warm solidity of Lysander's chest. All he did was hold her close and stroke her hair, but that was exactly what she needed. She knew she was making a damp, salty patch on his shirt yet she went on clinging to him, trying to put off the moment when she would have to apologise for falling apart on him.

Lysander was in no hurry to let her go. He lowered his head until it rested against hers. Sliding his hands around her body, he drew her closer. Her breathing slowed as she tried to decide what was happening, and what she wanted to do about it. Lysander was holding her in a way that Jerry had never done—like a true friend. It was a lovely, safe feeling and so far outside her experience she felt happy and scared at the same time.

'I'm sorry,' she sniffled at last.

'Don't be. You're so brave and kind and resourceful it comes as a relief to find you're human after all. I was beginning to think you had supernatural powers.' He chuckled, still holding her gently against him.

With the side of her face pressed against his chest, she felt his words as much as heard them. 'That's a wonderful thing to say. Thank you, Lysander.'

'It's my pleasure.'

Alyssa could believe it, from the way his arms were wrapped around her. She could have stayed like that for ever, but knew if she gave herself up to him now she could say goodbye to her independence. That frightened her. If she lost control and surrendered to her desires now, the inevitable would happen. Lysander would be the one calling the shots. His reputation as a womaniser made her determined not to melt, however strong her urge to become liquid beneath the firm pressure of his hands. Her confidence had been so badly battered, she didn't want to open all her old wounds again. She wanted Lysander, but not simply as a sleeping partner. Her feelings for him ran so much deeper and stronger than the indistinct fantasies of white lace and babies she had known with Jerry. Her need for Lysander was a hot, passionate desire, seething through her veins like liquid gold. She wanted him body and soul, or not at all. If she couldn't have the whole man, she had to resist the only part of him on offer tonight.

Determined to make her point, she moved. It was a wrench, but she forced herself to pull away from him.

'This is a first for me. Standing in a queen's garden, in a prince's arms!' she said, making herself chuckle.

He released her, slowly and gently. When he looked down into her face now, his dark eyes were glowing. 'It's a novelty to find someone who isn't desperate for me to do anything more than this. I never usually touch a woman without an ulterior motive.'

He spoke carefully, but after what she had been through Alyssa knew better than to expect too much in the way of real support from any man. She took a deep breath and tried to compose herself.

'You were comforting me. That was reason enough.' She gave a watery chuckle.

'Yes. And tonight it's the only motive I need,' he whispered, before pulling her back into his arms and kissing her until the sky went dark.

CHAPTER EIGHT

ALYSSA couldn't fight her feelings any more. When Lysander released her, she was so breathless with desire she couldn't speak either. It didn't matter. There weren't enough words to describe the way she felt. When he claimed her mouth with his own a second time, she sank into his arms without a care in the world. She had waited so long to feel the touch of his lips against hers again. Every fantasy flew from her mind as she relaxed into the total experience of his kisses. This was so much better than dreaming. The whole sensation of his body cradling hers and the touch of his tongue against her teeth, teasing the soft warm recesses of her mouth, was beyond wonderful. She was fully aware now that every second since she'd first laid eyes on Lysander had been leading up to this moment. The anticipation grew within her body, waiting to be satisfied by his expert touch...

Lysander knew this would be unlike any other lovemaking. The time for waiting was over. No woman had ever made him suffer like Alyssa. When she walked into his life with her beautiful body and her determined resistance to him, she had become a challenge he couldn't ignore. When she revealed her tragic past salted with tears, there had been no way he could fail to be moved. And now the touch of her peppermint-cool lips against his own… It was sublime. Everything about her was so much better than his fantasies. She surpassed all the women he had seduced before. He wanted to take his time, and make these moments last for ever so that each movement in the concerto of their desire would be turned into something special. Alyssa would be no ordinary conquest. He could feel her whole body tremble at his touch. He drew her close, and sent his fingers rippling up and down her spine. She gave a little moan of pleasure. That made him smile. She had brought him so many new experiences since they first met. Now it was time to take things to a whole new level for them both. Anticipation smouldered within him, turning his voice into pure temptation.

'Once upon a time you were afraid I might be able to read your mind. Does it worry you that I could be plundering your thoughts right now?'

'Mmm…but I know you aren't.' Her reply was low with desire. 'You're too kind to do it without asking.'

'Other women will tell you differently.'

'My common sense has been warning me off from the moment you burst into my life, Lysander. Tonight, I can't resist you any more.' She sighed, moving her cheek rhythmically against his. His skin was stippled with stubble, and teased her with a thousand points of pleasure.

'Alyssa, you drive me wild…'

'Good, so it's your turn to suffer,' she murmured

deep into his ear. 'Bringing me to the world's most romantic place to tempt me like this—'

'You deserve it.'

He nuzzled her ear, his words sending warm shivers of excitement right through her body. Nibbling down her neck until he reached her blouse, he dragged it aside with his teeth.

The thin fabric was no match for him. Alyssa gasped as one side of it fell away. Now there was nothing but a filigree of lacy bra between her left breast and his gaze.

'This is so wrong,' she breathed.

'Not if it's what you truly want…' His voice was running on pure testosterone.

Her answer was one long, wordless moan of longing. Lysander took her in his arms for a kiss that set her body on fire. She melted into his caresses until they were engulfed in pure, hot passion. This was like nothing she had ever experienced before. There was no room for thought, only action—Lysander's action.

'I can send you right up among those stars and planets, making you forget everything but the pleasure of my body, and yours. Is that what you want?' he asked, the earthy vibration of his voice almost more than she could bear.

Her fingernails drew tracks through his thick dark hair, pulling his head still closer.

'Yes…yes!'

'Then I will make love to you until every celestial light goes out…' he whispered, his breath dancing over her skin.

* * *

It was exactly as Lysander promised. Beneath that moonlit sky with its scatter of a few diamond stars, he made love to her in the most perfect sense of the word. Again and again her cries of exultation rang out into the desert night.

Finally, when pleasure had drained every sound from her, Lysander lowered his head to sip one last kiss from her lips. With it came a final question.

'Now?'

She looked up at him, sated with desire and wanting only his pleasure. The flickering firelight that danced in his eyes ignited her smile.

He exploded with a cry of ecstasy that echoed around the ancient walls of the observatory like a song. Alyssa arched to accept his body as wave after wave of pure pleasure carried them both beyond thought.

'Perfect—absolutely perfect,' he whispered when it was over, resting his cheek gently against her shoulder. Alyssa couldn't speak. There were no words to tell him how she felt, how he had made her feel. Instead, she rolled her head until she could bury her face in the soft, sweet smelling luxuriance of his dark hair.

'This is how it should be. Always,' she said, waiting for him to answer.

But he said nothing.

Lysander had lost track of time, of place, of everything. His whole existence contracted into The Queen's Retreat, a place that had unexpectedly come to represent everything good about life. Alyssa intrigued him with her independence. From the moment she walked into his life, her quiet, well ordered way of doing things had become a calm centre in the whirlpool of his new existence. She knew what she wanted, and now she had surrendered to him. As they lay together, his arms protecting her from the chill of the desert night, he smiled, and then wondered why. This seduction was supposed to defuse his desire for her, but it wasn't going to plan. Hours and hours after first contact, his need for her still burned as hot as ever. He consoled himself that the feeling would pass, eventually. It always did. He had made love to more women that he could remember, but their attraction never lasted beyond bed. Alyssa would be no different. She couldn't be. Last night she had been at a low ebb, and he merely stepped in to comfort her in the best way he knew how. There was nothing more to it than that.

The lust rising within him this instant, as her supple sleeping body moulded itself to his, was nothing more than a reaction to the warm pressure of her naked skin.

Sympathy for her is the only reason I'm not back in my own suite at the palace right now, he told himself. Not even Lysander was immune to hearing about a woman being abandoned by a rat of a fiancé. It was no wonder he was still here. How could he leave her so soon after learning about her tragic past? Alyssa was hurting because a man she had trusted had betrayed her.

Lysander might have specialised in having a new lover every night, but at least he was honest with them. They all knew better than to accept commitment from him. Alyssa was no exception—she had never made any secret of the fact that she didn't trust him an inch. That should have made him feel better. *This pity event was nothing more than a comfort to make her feel better,* he assured himself. *She'll understand.*

But would she?

He turned the matter over in his mind. She was a sensible woman, who knew his past. There could never be anything more than sex between a woman like her, and a man with his reputation. That should be obvious to anyone. Alyssa was far too down-to-earth to have any illusions, wasn't she? A night with him was guaranteed to make her forget her pain, and it would get his head back together, too. That was all. They were both level-headed people, and after these few supreme hours of satisfaction the two of them would plunge straight back into their totally respectable careers, and move on. After all, they both used their work as a substitute for adult relationships, and Alyssa worked as hard as he did. Those two facts united them against the world. He knew she was bound to feel the same way as he did about this incredible evening.

Nobody expects a one-night stand to create any emotional baggage, do they? Lysander thought, convincing himself there wouldn't be any fallout. Like him, Alyssa would write off this escapade as nothing more than a pleasant little blip for them both.

Wouldn't she?

Through the hours of darkness, Lysander spent a miraculous time giving Alyssa all the physical comfort any woman could ever need. They got no more sleep that night than the nightingales. They made love continuously beneath the golden moon, breathing in the intoxicating scent of the Queen's garden. It was only when they rested that Lysander had time to work on his excuses. *I'm only doing what she wants. It doesn't matter, as long as she's calling the shots. She's known what I'm like, from the start...*

'People will be wondering where you are,' Alyssa told him sleepily early next morning. She was stroking his hair as he lay with his head resting against her neck.

Lysander was safe in the knowledge he could walk away from her at any time, but that time wasn't now. It was a shame to stop her doing something that made her so happy.

'Let them wonder. And as it's your day off, I don't have to get you back to the Rose Palace until midnight tonight. We can stay here having fun for as long as we like,' he murmured drowsily.

'I shall need some clothes!' She giggled.

'Not for anything I have planned.'

It was his own sleepy reply that shocked Lysander wide awake. He was supposed to be escaping to check his emails and chair a steering committee. Having fun with naked women wasn't supposed to feature on his agenda any more.

Drawing his body away from hers, he got up. He felt Alyssa shiver at the loss of him, and was aware of her moving to try to see what he was doing.

'There's something wrong, Lysander. What is it? Can I help?'

Her concern brought him up short. A woman who was *really* interested in him as a person, not a bank balance? That made a change. It gave him a sense of security he had never felt in the presence of a girl before. He paused, and thought about her question before answering.

'No. I'm fine.'

Knowing he could have dropped everything and gone straight back into her arms was faintly worrying.

Groping among their scattered clothes for his mobile, he distracted himself by making a quick call.

'Breakfast will be served as soon as they can get it here,' he told her when he had finished.

'I'm hungry for only one thing, Lysander.'

'Me too,' he murmured, pulling her into his arms. 'That's why I'm taking you outside to the arbour, for one last experience before my staff gets here.'

It was a long time later when they wandered in to breakfast, through the swell of sweet-smelling flowers that filled the queen's garden. The old building had been transformed again. The table had been cleared and laid with fresh fruit and pastries, while changes of clothes were laid neatly over the back of a couch.

'After breakfast I'll show you the spa. It's a natural feature fed by hot springs, and it's the only luxury in the place.'

'You're my luxury, Lysander.' Alyssa blushed, adding quickly, 'I'm sorry about last night. The crying, I mean.'

'Those were unique circumstances,' he said brusquely. 'Don't worry about a thing.'

'You're right.' Her voice was small.

'Deep down you'll never forget the reason for those tears, but the pain will pass.' Lysander looked uncomfortable, and she saw he was making himself speak when he would rather have stayed silent.

She nodded.

He draped a robe carefully around her shoulders, then put one on himself. Sitting down on the nearest couch, he stared at their laden breakfast table.

'This is the first time I've ever envied my brother Akil. He was always much more sensitive than I am when it comes to women—at least until he took the cure.'

'What was that?' Alyssa enquired, puzzled.

'He got married.'

'Oh, dear!' Trying to laugh, she poured him a cup of coffee. Last night had been a spectacular experience, and she wanted it to last as long as possible. Despite all her fantasies, Jerry's treachery and her broken engagement had taught her that happiness was painfully short-lived. She knew that the sooner they parted today, the faster Lysander's interest in her would die.

He accepted the cup and helped himself to a couple of pebbles of unrefined sugar. They took a long time to dissolve, and for a while the only sound was the gentle caress of his silver spoon against the bone china cup. Alyssa was determined not to ask any more questions unless he wanted to talk.

'You don't share my curiosity about people, then?' he said after his first sip.

'As I said, I meant to do some online research in my spare time to get background, but now I know what happened to your mother I'm not sure I want to know anything more about your family. Unless it would help my work with Ra'id, of course,' she said without looking at him. It was enough to feel his eyes watching her every move, stripping her soul bare in the same way he had removed her inhibitions during that spectacular desert night.

'Of course,' he said, then muttered another word in Rosari that Alyssa was glad she couldn't understand.

'For one thing, it was useful to find out that Ra'id isn't the only candidate for King,' she said carefully.

He didn't reply straight away. Alyssa tensed. Watching him wonder how much to tell her was almost as bad as imagining this strong, capable man pacing about his state rooms like the caged tiger he had talked about.

'History has a way of repeating itself, but I'm not going to recreate the mistakes of the past,' he said grimly. 'Times change, but mankind stays the same. Loving too much killed my mother. She may have been in the wrong, but the people of Rosara hated the way she was treated. Father was determined things would change. He even allowed my brother to marry for love, rather than selecting a bride for him. Of course, that didn't work out any better than the traditional system of an arranged marriage,' he said with obvious disgust. 'While he was King, Akil continued to make improvements to Rosara. Now it's all been left to me. Life was so much simpler when my father or Akil did the work and I was left to enjoy myself! There's not much joy in juggling guardianship, running a country and making sure the succession doesn't rely on Ra'id alone.'

'It's such a shame he doesn't have any brothers or sisters.'

Alyssa sighed.

'His parents' marriage had already broken down before he was born. My brother thought marriage should be for ever, so, although he eventually let me convince him to separate from Ra'id's mother, he refused to consider fathering more children with another woman. He was old-fashioned enough to think that would set a bad example to his country.'

'And of course he never expected to die before Ra'id was old enough to take over. That's such a shame.' Alyssa clicked her tongue. 'Things would have been so different, if only the late king had remarried and had more children.'

'So you don't think marriage should be for ever?' Lysander placed his cup down, carefully matching its base to the small depression in his saucer so he didn't have to look at her.

'Of course I do—but things don't always work out so well in the real world.'

Lysander hunched his shoulders in weary resignation.

'How long were you engaged?' he asked quietly.

'Just over three years.'

Naked astonishment wiped the last trace of anger from his face. 'Good God! What was *wrong* with the man?'

Alyssa thought for a while before answering. She had only just started to admit the truth to herself. It was hard to know whether sharing it with Lysander would be a good idea. Her feelings were still so delicate. Admitting that she had slipped into the relationship because it was a step on the way to achieving her dreams rather than her ideal destination would be hard.

'It wasn't his fault, it was mine,' she said eventually, and was overcome by a great rush of relief. She had done it. Now the dam was breached, she could let a whole torrent of words follow.

'I was in love with the idea of love. My working life was filled with other people's babies and children, and I enjoyed it all so much I couldn't wait to start a family of my own. In my fantasy world they would adore me, and shower me with all the affection I'd never had from my parents. When I met Jerry, he fitted my identikit picture of an ideal father. He was solid, hardworking and had his future as an accountant all mapped out—complete with career database, objectives, the lot! My parents were so impressed by him, it spilled over to me—finally I had their approval. I was on top of the world, looking forward to the wedding of the century, and starting the perfect family.

'Then little Georgie died and as I fell apart, so did our relationship. We didn't have enough in common to sustain it. Jerry couldn't understand why Georgie's death hit me so hard. I couldn't explain that the grief was bad enough, but knowing that I could have done more to save him made it ten times worse...'

Her voice broke. Lysander grabbed his clean jacket, and pulled a neatly pressed handkerchief from its breast pocket. He pushed it into Alyssa's hands. She thanked him with a smile, but her eyes were dry.

'When we couldn't talk about it, Jerry lost interest in me,' she continued. 'Not long after that, he broke off our engagement. That was when I found out he'd been messing around with one of his office juniors for quite a while.' Expecting to need Lysander's handkerchief at any second, she squeezed it into a thousand creases.

The tears didn't come, because there weren't any left. *This really must be the beginning of a new chapter in my life*, she thought.

'I know exactly how you must feel.'

If anyone else had said that to her, Alyssa would have bitten their heads off for being patronising. When it came to Lysander, she knew that wasn't what he intended. His life was full of flings. That meant he could put more understanding into his words than there had been in the whole of her long engagement. It would have been funny, if it weren't so sad.

'I hated Jerry for doing that, but now I can see there were faults on both sides. I was only using him as a way to get the life I'd always wanted.'

'So you lost the chance to bag the rich husband of your dreams?' Lysander replied in a flat voice.

'That was the last thing on my mind when I looked at Jerry. I've got my own career—why would I be interested in his money? It's not as though I'd need to pay for childcare...' She tried to laugh, but couldn't do it. 'Looking back, I can see now that I agreed to marry him only because he asked me, not because of anything he could give me beyond children.'

Lysander picked up a plate from the table and offered her a ripe fig as a peace offering. It was so sweet compared to her memories. She savoured it for as long as possible. Then Lysander handed her a finger bowl and a soft, scented towel for her hands.

'And there was another problem.' She warmed to her theme. 'As an accountant, Jerry worked long hours. He had no interest in my work, and the feeling was mutual. I didn't have the first thing in common with any of the other accountants' wives and fiancées, either.'

'Yes. I can imagine,' Lysander said darkly. 'I've met a few of those at the parties we've held for firms who work for us. The best trophy wives don't seem to have an independent thought between them.' He smiled, until Alyssa had to join in.

'Or careers,' she added. 'I liked my life the way it was…but then it all went wrong.'

'The other woman.' Lysander sighed with world-weary certainty.

'Yes—and the worst of it was, I might never have found out if it hadn't been for what happened to Georgie.'

'Your loss must have been devastating,' Lysander said quietly.

Alyssa nodded, hardly expecting Lysander to be any more understanding than her ex-fiancé.

'For that little boy to die of meningitis was the worst possible tragedy. For everyone around to have ignored your warnings until it was too late must have struck you so hard.'

She looked at him, glad that tears still felt a long way off. 'You make me sound like a control freak.'

'I wouldn't go as far as that, but I *have* noticed you share a stubborn streak with my late brother. Wait—that's not necessarily a bad thing!' Lysander added as she got ready to fly off the handle. 'Akil's rigid determination was a great asset in a king, but not so good in a human being. Some things about you remind me of him. He never knew when to relax, be more flexible and let go.'

'Which is something *you* can do better than anyone else in the world,' Alyssa rejoined sharply, a little wounded by his quick assessment. 'How can a man like you ever feel comfortable in the role of regent, let alone king?'

A quick flash of consciousness in Lysander's eyes showed that her shaft had hit its mark, but a moment later he had smoothed his expression out and answered blandly:

'I intend to continue my brother's work, not his life choices.' The dark eyes took on a more thoughtful depth. 'Alyssa, I wanted to ask you something as a newcomer to the country. Have you heard any rumours about my late sister-in-law's affairs?'

Alyssa's eyes widened. 'No...what are you suggesting? That Ra'id may not be Akil's son?'

Lysander gave her a long, steady look. 'You catch on fast. But remember—you said it, not me. It's another good reason why our country is entering a troubled time—the power of the rebels continues to grow. It's not dangerous yet, but I must take as much responsibility for Rosara as the people want to give me.'

Alyssa gazed back at him, wondering if that was the reason he had kept his distance from Ra'id until he took her to the nursery in person on that first day. It must have been so difficult for Lysander to have lost his brother, and then be forced to care for a child that might be no blood relation at all, and nothing more than a cuckoo in the Kahani nest.

Then she saw something about Lysander's dark eyes that reminded her of Ra'id. They were so alike…

That was when she felt her own eyes getting bigger and rounder by the second.

Lysander noticed, and made an irritable noise in the back of his throat. 'Alyssa! If I hadn't become hardened to all the gossip years ago, I would be very offended by that look.'

'I never said a thing!' she retorted, ashamed he could read her thoughts so easily.

'You didn't need to.' He clapped his hand loudly to his chest. 'But I'm blameless in that direction, if no other. I never laid a finger on my late sister-in-law, nor ever wanted to. You have my word on that.'

He looked so genuine, Alyssa couldn't help but believe him. 'I'm sorry, Lysander. I shouldn't have judged you,' she said, then rallied: 'Although don't forget, you only took offence because you were searching my mind through my eyes.'

His reply was quicksilver. 'I do it because I can't help keeping a *very* close check on them, all the time.'

'And I thought your mind was supposed to be full of nothing but work!'

'You've been in danger of eclipsing that for me from the first moment we met.'

His voice was like a breeze through cool ferns. Alyssa was hypnotised by his dark stare, feeling as well as seeing it travel to her lips. Then, with a sigh full of regret, he looked away from her.

'My country is my work, and nothing can be allowed to distract me any more. Nothing. Although I will show you something that comes very close…'

As he took her hand such a powerful thrill of excitement ran through her body he must have felt it. Drawing her out into the garden again, he looked back at her over his shoulder. In that moment, his expression almost stopped her heart completely.

'Dawn in my country is as spectacular as the full moon,' he whispered.

Alyssa could believe it—as long as she was sharing it with him.

Helping her up to the highest lookout point on the castle walls, he sheltered her with his body against any chill breeze off the desert. The rising sun was already staining the Eastern sky with colours of pomegranate and peach. Down in the gardens, nightingales still sang. Their music was a grace note for Alyssa's perfect fantasy, and she relaxed into Lysander's embrace. No woman had ever felt so adored. As she felt his kisses on her hair and looked out over the ageless scene she allowed herself to imagine being this happy for ever.

Then without warning she was woken from her beautiful dream. A tiny sound had begun, far out in the desert. It grew faster than the daybreak, careering towards their happiness. Lysander was the first to realise what it was. While Alyssa was still wondering, he stiffened and pushed her gently away from him. The cold morning air flooded the space between them. Needing his closeness, she followed as he went to stand with his hands on the coping stones of the castle wall.

He was intent on something far out across the sands. A vehicle was hurtling at breakneck speed over the hard-packed desert. With growing horror, Alyssa saw that their paradise was about to be wrecked. Suddenly

Lysander strode away from her, back down the steps the way they had come. She ran to catch up, breathless with fear now, rather than expectation.

'What is it, Lysander?'

'For someone to be heading this way so fast, it must be a message from the palace.'

His words were terse and businesslike. Alyssa stopped. Lysander didn't notice, and certainly didn't wait for her. His mind was miles away, already centred on his work. This realisation sent her powering after him again. She knew what it was like to be driven, and wanted to share the responsibility with him.

'What can I do?' she called, but it was no good. He was completely absorbed by the arrival of a big new four-by-four in the blue and gold palace livery.

The vehicle skidded to a halt in the courtyard and the driver jumped out. Hustling the man out of her earshot, Lysander began an animated exchange with him. Alyssa could only stand by and watch. They spoke in Rosari, so she had no hope of understanding more than a fraction of what they were saying. From the speed at which the message was delivered, she guessed it was bad news. When the messenger jumped back into the vehicle and started gunning the engine, Lysander strode back to where she waited for an explanation.

It didn't come.

'I'm sorry about this.'

'You have to go,' she said, her voice as flat as the plain that isolated them from real life.

'Yes.'

'But you'll come back to me?'

He stared at her as though she were the one speaking

a foreign language. Then he lifted his gaze to look at the sky. She couldn't help wondering if it was for inspiration.

The rising sun was now high enough to light his face. Reaching out, he took her by the shoulders.

'I must get straight back to the palace now. I'll try to call on you later.'

His words pushed all the air out of her lungs. Logically, she knew that their time together was only fleeting, but somehow she had expected the pleasure to last a little longer than this before the pain kicked in.

'Are you expecting me to count the minutes?' she said in a bitter undertone as he turned his back on her.

It was one tiny act of defiance, a kick against the tomorrow she could not avoid. She didn't expect him to either hear, or care. When he turned and pierced her with a look, she froze. She could do nothing but watch as he prowled back across the courtyard towards her. Her thudding heart counted down the seconds until he was towering over her, his eyes brilliant with something she had never seen in them before. Ice ran through her veins as he leaned close…and then closer still. The warmth of his breath rippling over the delicate skin of her face and neck caressed an unwilling excitement over her body. A flush suffused the pale skin of her cleavage as she became aware that he was awakening her nipples to hard peaks all over again. Dimly aware of his hand moving past the corner of her eye, she tensed. Extending one lean, tanned finger, he pushed a stray skein of hair back from her brow. From there, his finger traced a leisurely path around the curve of her cheek. When he reached her chin, he lifted it so she was compelled to meet his eyes again.

'Yes.'

CHAPTER NINE

LYSANDER'S voice was low and rough, but this time he studied her lips with cool, professional interest. Alyssa held her breath. Her heart pounded on. She wondered if he could hear it, amplified as it was by the powerful surge of desire thundering through her body. As he brought his head nearer and nearer to her, she watched until she was dizzy with desire. Then her eyes closed. She waited one…two seconds, but the kiss she was aching for never came. Instead she felt him take her hand. Her eyes flew open again. She saw his dark head bent over her fingers at the moment his lips brushed her skin in the lightest of formal gestures. Alyssa was so aroused, a little moan of longing escaped from her lips. A heat far more powerful than all the strength of the sun turned her body to a molten mass. It was frightening—almost as frightening as his smouldering gaze.

The memory of everything they had shared brought her straight back into the present. All that pleasure had been swept from his face and his manner, and now he was preparing for business as usual. He looked every inch the king. Alyssa couldn't imagine what had possessed her to tell him to concentrate on Ra'id rather than his own chances for the crown of Rosara.

'Yes…you must go, Lysander,' she told him, but the meaning in her voice was far more powerful than her words.

He let her hand slip from his grasp. As his expressive dark eyes held her captive he placed one finger on the soft cushion of her lips. Tracing their outline with a touch as light as thistledown, he watched her fight the temptation to reach out and start caressing him again. She still wanted him, and her attraction grew like a flower. She might try to hide it, but her unsteady breathing and dilated pupils told Lysander everything. His own perfectly sculpted mouth fluctuated into a smile.

'I'm sorry,' he drawled. 'Duty must come first.'

Kiss me! Alyssa's body sobbed silently.

She reached up, wanting to ruffle her fingers through his soft dark curls once more before he left. He responded by pulling her close, moulding her body against his own so she could feel how much he wanted her, how much his body would like to stay.

'Take care, my love,' she whispered.

His hands had been running over her back, shoulders and hair. When she said that, he stopped and drew back. His eyes were now filled with a watchful look that frightened her.

'I'm always careful. Very careful.'

Cupping her shoulders with his hands, he interrogated her with a long, cool look. Alyssa returned it with a smile. She knew he could read her mind, but this time his expression was closed to her.

'Lysander? What is it?' She put her hands up to his

face again, but was too slow. He had already broken contact with her and was turning towards the car.

'Nothing. I hope.'

He dived into the four-by-four and rapped on the dashboard as a signal to the driver. In a crash of gears, Lysander was swept away from her in a squeal of burning rubber.

Alyssa waved as the vehicle became a comet at the head of a dust cloud, but he never once looked back.

A bleak, black mood enveloped Lysander. He was used to playing dangerous games, but now he had been ambushed into doing something unforgivable. He had planned the perfect seduction to cure his gnawing need for Alyssa. Instead, raw emotion had overwhelmed them both and made the situation much, much worse. Alyssa's silent, hidden vulnerability touched him. Her tears had been an unexpected tidal wave, washing away all his defences. What else could he have done, but take her in his arms and make everything all right again in the only way he knew how?

He watched her image in the nearside wing mirror. It shrank until it was hidden by the swirling dust thrown up by his vehicle. He could only hope she was every inch the woman he believed her to be. She was so unlike all the others…she was bound to understand, wasn't she? Like him, she knew from hard, horrible experience that long-term relationships were impossible.

They were both free spirits. That would help. When she had burst into tears last night, it had been only a simple mistake on her part—he had put that right and solved his own problem, too. The last thing he should have done was start to feel genuinely sorry for her. That was his mistake, but it was understandable.

When he thought about it like that, his lapse didn't feel quite so bad. He dropped his hand onto his thigh and relaxed his shoulders. All he had intended was a quick tumble in a beautiful place. Offering Alyssa sympathy had been delicious, but he had never wanted to get in so deep. Sex was supposed to be fun, not serious. That was why this call back to the palace was such a godsend.

Uneasily, he realised abandoning Alyssa this morning for anything less would have been impossible. That made things tricky. An affair wouldn't be right for either of them. Lysander was certain of that, in the same way he knew he would have to get Alyssa right out of his life as soon as possible—to save his sanity.

Alyssa ran back up the steps to the lookout point on top of the castle walls. From there she could watch Lysander's car and its thread of dust fade from sight across the plain. When it had disappeared into the low jumble of buildings making up the palace, she turned and headed for the spa. There, she stripped off and slipped beneath the warm waters. Her spirits soared up to the clear blue sky, exhilarating, yet terrifying. She had wasted so much time mourning her broken engagement, it had blinded her.

It was far more than simply desire she felt for Lysander.

When Lysander got back to the palace he blazed his way through the corridors of power. *I should never have abandoned my work. I should have come straight back here last night,* he told himself, but it was hopeless to deny the attraction that had held him prisoner at The Queen's Retreat for so long. He had been bedding Ra'id's nanny when he should have been putting his country first. Now his past and future were on a collision course. A rowdy faction of hill tribes was on its way to the palace, ready to proclaim their own King of Rosara, rather than wait for his nephew to grow up.

Lysander's word was already law to them. He was confident that he could control the situation, but that didn't make it any easier. When Alyssa got to hear of this, she was bound to be scared. He already knew how good she was at hiding her feelings, but he had just spent a whole night breaking down her resistance. This situation meant he had to focus. It was time to let her go, like all the others.

But she wasn't like them. And what if Ra'id picked up on the atmosphere this was bound to create? How would *that* affect their working relationship? If they still had one…

His veins ran with ice water as he remembered how Alyssa had mentioned the L word—love. He knew what that meant. Seduction might not have slaked his thirst for her, but when a woman used words like that it had to mean the end of everything. There was no question about it. When love came in the door, common sense flew out of the window. He had too much experience of that, and it was a painful experience. It had condemned his mother to death, and broken his brother's heart. Lysander had to prove he was bigger than either of them. There was only one way to do it—make a clean break from Alyssa while he worked things out in his mind.

He would double the guard on Ra'id and go to intercept the rebels on their own ground. He was interested in results for Rosara, not in honour for himself. Alyssa would understand that. He could tell that the country was beginning to hold almost the same importance for her as it did for him…

Suddenly, he realised it wasn't going to be easy to prise his thoughts away from her. If her voluptuous image could haunt him while he was preparing for a council of war, he didn't know how it could be exorcised. He had to send her away.

The Queen's Retreat was a beautiful place to idle away her day off, but Alyssa soon got restless. After Lysander's lovemaking, everything else was second best. Life felt almost impossible without him now. Lounging in a swing seat beneath the rose arbour, she hummed to herself. A billow of single pink daisies flounced around the trellis. Picking one as she rocked gently to and fro, she began pulling off the narrow petals one by one.

'He loves me, he loves me not…'

Going through the old rhyme felt deliciously wicked. Princes weren't supposed to carry their staff away into the desert. Nannies ought to concentrate on the next generation, not fool around with men of their own age.

She went on reciting the rhyme until there were only six petals left.

'He loves me…'

A commotion far away in the palace's gatehouse

made her stop. She listened, and then suddenly a guard was running across the courtyard, calling to her. She couldn't understand what he was saying, but recognised the sound of her own name.

Whatever the news, it wasn't good. She looked down at the flower in her hand, with its half-dozen remaining petals.

'Miss Dene! You are recalled to the palace!' the man called to her in broken English. 'Prince Lysander insisted that you were sent for. Your day off is cancelled! You must take the child back to England immediately!'

'Isn't Prince Lysander coming back to fetch me himself?'

'No, he's far too busy!' The guard sounded shocked, as if Alyssa was the last thing on the Prince Regent's mind. She tensed.

'Why? What's happened?'

'The time has come. Prince Lysander is going to confront the rebels and Prince Ra'id's household is all going back to England, where they'll be safe.'

Alyssa took the news like a blow to the stomach. The queen's garden was suddenly full of people. They swarmed around her like ants, emptying the observatory of all the lovely things she had enjoyed with Lysander. She stood in the eye of the storm, her mind already a maelstrom. Opening her hand, she looked down at the daisy that had been giving her so much innocent pleasure.

A quick calculation told her everything she didn't want to know. She pinched five petals together and pulled them off. That left only one.

He loves me not...

So there it was. Not even a child's game worked in her favour any more. She couldn't manage to keep that final, fragile petal, either. It was snatched out of her fingers by a chill breeze rippling across the garden.

For a moment, all the birds fell silent.

Lysander had been so understanding about Georgie's death and Jerry's treachery, but his silver tongue had lured her into making another mistake. Alyssa shut her eyes, trying to blind herself to the truth in the same way he had done. It was impossible. She was as big a fool as ever. Bigger, as experience should have taught her not to be so stupid a second time. She had allowed herself to be seduced, knowing all the time that Lysander's lifestyle and morals were totally different from her own. Her ex-fiancé had cheated on her while she was still grieving for Georgie, and when she had needed him most. Why should she be shocked when ruthless, single-minded Lysander Kahani did exactly the same?

She stood up. The remains of the daisy, already wilting in the warmth, tumbled from her lap. She didn't notice. All she could think about was the way she had made a fool of herself over a man—again.

A car came for her, eventually, but there was no sign of Lysander. When she got back to the Rose Palace, it was in chaos. Lysander was nowhere to be seen but she couldn't block out the sound of his voice, calm but loud, echoing through the building. Staff scurried about all day relaying his instructions, and she picked up the story bit by bit. Lysander was leaving with the army for the hills. His plan was to make contact with the rebels who had sent an ultimatum about Ra'id. To keep his nephew safe, the royal household was being shipped back to England. Alyssa didn't want Ra'id upset by all the tension, so she kept him in the nursery, but the last thing she wanted to do was merge into the background.

For once, she was determined to stand up for herself. She had to talk to Lysander. Although her attention didn't waver from Ra'id, she made sure they always played close to a window where she could keep a watch on the courtyard below. Lysander didn't appear. She texted him. He didn't reply. All day she watched and waited, but it was no good. Finally, with Ra'id packed and ready, she had an excuse to go and find out what was happening.

The palace's grand foyer was stacked with travelling boxes and crates. Alyssa spotted Lysander instantly. The sight of him stopped her dead, halfway down the stairs. He was always impressive, but in combats instead of his usual designer suit and tie he was daunting as well. In contrast to his staff, he moved around with cool assurance. They rushed backwards and forwards in a panic while he tried to keep the situation calm by giving each one a few reassuring words.

Alyssa waited for him to turn his head so she could attract his attention. He didn't so much as throw a glance towards her. When anger overcame her shame at being fooled twice in her life, she started down the stairs. Each step was heavier than the last. When she finally thumped to ground level, Lysander was heading towards the door.

'I'd like a word with you, please, Your Royal Highness.'

The staff stopped, guessed what was going to happen

and then put their heads down to carry on with what they were doing.

All except Lysander. Hands on hips and without any sense of urgency, he strolled over to where she stood.

Alyssa's face barely came up to his breast pocket, but that didn't stop her standing up to him.

'I want to speak to you.'

'I know. I saw you leave the nursery wing.'

That surprised her. 'You didn't make any effort to come over while I was waiting on the stairs,' she snapped, feeling awkward that she had misjudged him. Only hours ago, she had felt there might be some kind of mystical link growing between them. *Fat chance, when I can't even notice him looking at me*, she thought.

'Is it something about Ra'id?' His eyes were guarded.

'No.'

'What, then?'

'You mean you don't know?' Alyssa burst out.

He stood before her, tall, proud and very still. 'I hope I can't guess.'

Now that she was face to face with him, Alyssa couldn't think of how to begin. Eventually, she said in a quiet voice, 'I thought you were coming back to The Queen's Retreat.'

'I was needed here.'

'Of course you were.' Alyssa had heard about threats to Ra'id's future from the driver sent to collect her. The country was unsettled, angry, looking for a strong leader. There were bound to be those who might want to take a short cut by removing any opposition. That put Ra'id quite literally into the firing line.

She fought to keep calm. Only twenty-four hours ago the three of them had been having a wonderful time, picnicking without a care in the world. Now her universe had contracted to a tiny bubble that wasn't large enough to keep both Lysander and Ra'id safe at the same time. Bubbles were so easily burst. She would have to let one of them go, and Lysander wouldn't allow her to keep him. This was the job he was born to do, after all. She understood a sense of duty and how he felt about it, but this situation was so dangerous her feelings burst out in spite of herself.

'Please don't go, Lysander. Send someone else—'

A tiny muscle twitched as he clenched his jaw. 'Are you suggesting I should hide away, just so *you* aren't worried about my safety, when the future of both my country and my nephew are at stake?' The bitterness in his voice and his assumption that she was thinking only of herself cut through Alyssa like a whip.

'Don't flatter yourself—or me,' she struck back. 'Obviously my opinions aren't of any interest to you. How stupid of me to forget that for you women are nothing but playthings! Well, I'm worth more than that, and I'm not trying to save you for myself. See sense. If you're going to keep your country in one piece, Lysander, you have to keep yourself out of harm's way.'

'My country needs me to be strong, and I have to set an example. This is how it must be.'

'You idiot, Lysander!' Emotion made her throw her hands towards him but he stepped smartly out of her reach.

'Speaking like that to me at a time like this is treason.'

They stared at each other, his look becoming a glare.

'This will be my life from now on, Alyssa. There

are times when I have to leave everything—and everybody—behind. I can't do my duty to my people if I have you to worry about as well. There isn't room in my life for any distraction right now.'

Breath caught in her throat, almost choking her. 'So that's all I am to you—a distraction.'

He stared at a point somewhere over her head and far away. 'Don't take it to heart. If anything, you should be glad I'm leaving before things go any further. I've had so many other women, Alyssa. I've abandoned them all sooner or later—' He tore his eyes away from the middle distance but still refused to meet her eyes. 'I don't want to hurt you like that. You're too good…'

She took a step forward, daring him to flinch. 'You say that—but I was stupid enough to let you seduce me!' she blazed. 'You coward! You're walking away from me in the same way you've abandoned all those other girls over the years—to prove that you can. Don't deny it!' she spat furiously.

The look transforming his face told her she was right, but that he hadn't realised it himself until then. Seeing his sudden shock was unnerving. Lysander didn't notice. He was on an adrenaline high and struck back instantly.

'*I've* got nothing to prove!' he roared back. '*You're* the one whose future is on the line if you stay here. Go, now! It isn't safe for you here!'

'I'm going! But not because of anything you've said or done, Lysander Kahani,' she hissed. 'My first loyalty is to Ra'id. As far as I'm concerned, *you* can go to hell!'

'Good! That's exactly how it should be! I don't damn

well employ you to put me off my stroke!' he shouted over the racket of helicopters dropping onto the apron outside the palace, but it didn't make any difference to Alyssa. She was running back upstairs, desperate to get away from him.

Alyssa was in such turmoil she took refuge in organising. Packing and timetables were facts and figures she could control. Lysander might have thrown her on the scrapheap, but she had to bury that at the back of her mind. Ra'id was upset by all the confusion and change, and her first duty was always to him. Her own future looked bleak. The little boy was Lysander's number one fan, with all that meant. If he wasn't talking about his uncle, he was waiting for that one special visitor to the nursery. Alyssa would never be able to escape the influence of a man who had lifted her up and then dropped her from a great height.

The only silver lining was that, while she had so much to do for Ra'id, she didn't have time to get in a state about their hastily arranged flight home to England.

For the next few days, Alyssa spent her time trying to forget Lysander. It was impossible. By the time they got back to Combe House, the place was buzzing with news. Every bulletin started her fussing over Ra'id so she wouldn't have to hear, and bundling him away from every TV and radio. She said it was to stop the little boy getting upset. The truth was, she didn't know what would be worse: to hear that Lysander was in danger, or to find out that the emergency was all over and he was back home, looking for a new distraction. Either way, her heart would be pierced. Finally, the time came when she couldn't run any more. One morning she woke up while it was still dark outside to hear a television blaring away somewhere close at hand. Dragging on her dressing gown, she stumbled through the door connecting her suite with the nursery sitting room.

Ra'id was bouncing up and down on the couch, alight with excitement. He didn't notice that Alyssa's scowl would have curdled milk, and that she was pale with lack of sleep and loss of appetite. He had the TV on full blast, and launched straight into his great news.

'Uncle Ly's won!' he squealed with excitement.

'I've told you before not to switch the television on yourself!' she began, but Ra'id was far too excited to take any notice.

'Uncle Ly's won!' He kept on repeating it, but Alyssa couldn't bring herself to feel anything but dread. Ra'id's delight made it hard to pick out many details, but the words 'royal wedding' came through loud and clear as he pointed towards the giant TV screen. 'Now we can go home, and he can get married!'

Alyssa was shocked into life. She whirled around, and was confronted by Lysander's life-sized image moving over the huge TV screen. It twisted a knife in her stomach. His smile was exactly as she remembered; she could almost believe he was gazing straight at her. But he wasn't. He was sharing a joke with a rebel leader seated beside him at the conference table.

'He's getting married?' Alyssa's voice rose uncontrollably.

'Of course. He's going to marry Princess Peronelle.' Ra'id's smile reached from ear to ear.

Alyssa barely heard. She was frozen with horror, watching Lysander—the man who had cradled her, and made love to her until all her pain had gone. He was smiling and nodding wisely, ranks of photographers and film cameramen catching his every chuckle.

'He's…in love with a princess?' Alyssa felt faint. Suddenly the floor felt as if it were made from rubber. She caught hold of the nearest chair for support.

'Prince and princess, king and queen. That's how it goes,' Ra'id announced happily. 'The TV says King Boduan is sending Princess Peronelle on an official visit to Rosara as soon as Uncle Ly gets back there next week. It's inked,' Ra'id announced. He had picked up that delightful phrase parrot-fashion from one of Lysander's briefing team.

Alyssa was falling through space, helpless and alone. Her mouth was so dry she could hardly speak. 'Prince Lysander's going to get married?'

'I keep telling you. It's Princess Peronelle. *Everyone* knows that!' The little boy laughed.

'Since when? I didn't,' Alyssa said faintly, wondering how she could have been so deaf, blind and stupid.

'That's probably because it happened a long time ago,' Ra'id decided. 'I wasn't supposed to be listening. They thought I was playing. My father said Princess Peronelle had a good pedigree, whatever that is, but Uncle Ly said what good had that done our family in the past and that she was a…' he rolled his eyes with the effort of remembering '…a perfect clothes horse.'

A long time ago. So Lysander must *have known*

about his engagement before he carried me off to The
Queen's Retreat and...

Alyssa couldn't bear to think back over what had
happened. She had seen all those magazine photographs of Lysander escorting beautiful women around
the world. She knew the type only too well, but a hid-
eous need to know more about one in particular overwhelmed her.

'What's she like?'

The television coverage switched to other news, so
Rai'd lost interest in it. Instead of bouncing up and
down on the spot he was now catapulting from cushion to cushion along the length of the couch. Alyssa
had to repeat her question before he took any notice.

'The princess? She's not as nice as you.'

That made Alyssa feel worse, not better. The
only prize for coming second in the competition for
Lysander's love was a broken heart, and she already
had one of those.

'Have you met her?'

'Sort of. She came to the palace once. She walked
past me. She's all rustly, and smells like shops. She
didn't stop or talk to me or anything, but her ladies-
in-waiting did. They gave me sweets. Lots of sweets.
And chocolate. And marzipan. Lots of that, too. Then
we went into dinner and I was sick on the table and the
princess screamed and ran away.'

Alyssa might be dying inside, but that little picture
made her smile like a jealous jaguar.

'Oh, dear. Was it just on the table?'

Ra'id nodded.

'That was a shame,' Alyssa said with real feeling, but not the sort Princess Peronelle would have liked.

Lysander had some damned nerve, seducing me when he had a royal bride already lined up for himself, she thought, covering her face with her hands. *Now I know why he was so keen to send me back here without talking to me—I'd served my purpose.*

Despite everything, she felt strangely calm. Since Georgie died, she had always known that getting too fond of anyone was a mistake. So why had she let Lysander break her heart twice over? He had the words 'love rat' written all over him, he was fully aware of his own worth, and he was beautiful with it. She only had herself to blame for ignoring all the warning signs, but that couldn't stop her hating him.

'What's the matter? Have you got a pain?' Ra'id stopped bouncing and looked almost as stricken as Alyssa felt.

'Yes,' she said.

But she didn't tell him that pain was called Lysander Kahani.

CHAPTER TEN

THERE was no escape. From that moment on, Combe House was filled with talk about the forthcoming royal wedding. The newspapers seemed to know more than the staff did, so each morning a copy of every title was brought in. Everyone but Alyssa pored over them to discover the latest rumours. The ceremony was going to be held in the vast chapel at the Rose Palace in Rosara. All the talk was of which royal families and TV celebrities would be invited, what they would eat and which designer would be dressing the bride. Ra'id was so excited at the thought of his uncle Ly getting married, he talked about it non-stop. Egged on by the footmen, he decided he would be the official ring-bearer. His happy chatter wrecked every second of every day for Alyssa—until someone showed him the official photographs of his parents' wedding. Ra'id took one look at the lace encrusted, Rosari court dress their little page-boys had been forced to wear, and went strangely quiet.

Once he discovered how he would be dressed for the big occasion, Alyssa had no more trouble with Ra'id. He had spent hours trampling over her feelings and nagging to be involved. Now he couldn't wait to retreat with her to the spa wing. He didn't mention either Lysander, or the wedding, again.

Alyssa had to cope with his disappointment while keeping her own agony locked deep in her heart. Letting Ra'id fool around in the ball pit, she tried to drown her own sorrows in the warm, rose-perfumed waters of the Combe House pool. Whatever was happening back in Rosara, Lysander didn't want her any more. That simple fact drained all the life and hope out of her. She had never known a pain like it. What she was forced to endure now showed up her old heartbreak for what it was—a fuss over nothing but vanity. When Jerry had admitted his affair, she had felt viciously cheated of her big day and the happy ever after she assumed was her right—but that was all. She could see it now. Losing Jerry hadn't been the cause of all her anguish. Any feelings she might have had for him had shrivelled and died on the day he had told her to pull herself together after Georgie died. She deserved better, but looking back now she could see why Jerry had strayed. They had both been playing parts: hard-working professionals planning a safe, predictable future like all their so-called friends. It had been Alyssa's shattered dreams and damaged pride that had hurt the most. Jerry had almost been an optional extra in her plans for the perfect wedding.

The way she felt about Lysander had nothing to do with promises and party favours. She had known from the start he would have no interest in either, but for a little while he had been kind, and funny, and a spectacular lover. She had ignored all the pointers in his past and her own experience, and now she was paying the price. What more could she expect?

Despite everything, she found herself worrying as well as hurting. Whatever else he might have done, Lysander had listened, and comforted her. His own very special brand of kindness was impossible to forget. He had led a charmed life so far, but there was still a chance his luck would run out before he got back from his mission to the mountains. Alyssa couldn't bear to think of him being injured or killed. She knew she shouldn't care, but she did.

If he could seduce her while knowing about the plans for his arranged marriage, he must think she wasn't good enough for anything more than a bit part in his life. It hurt—but, thinking about it, she realised her parents and Jerry must have thought about her in much the same way.

It was a turning point. She had got over those disappointments. It felt as though she would *never* get over this, but there was one thing she could do to start on the road to recovery. If Lysander came back expecting to take up where he'd left off, he'd be out of luck. Alyssa's recent experiences had made her damned sure of one thing—she was too good to be nothing more than a mistress to him, and if she got the chance she wouldn't be afraid to say so.

The sound of an approaching microlight cut through her pain like a buzz saw. Rousing herself, she waded to the side of the pool. Ra'id always liked to be called out to see anything like that. As she climbed the steps a two-man machine swept low and slow over the trees surrounding Combe House. It swung around like an irritating horsefly, getting lower with every circuit. Alyssa was already angry and upset. She thought things couldn't possibly get worse—until she heard one of the riders call out to her. She looked up, and saw a long lens.

She ran to the ball pit to keep Ra'id inside the spa, but the damage was done. There could be only one reason why the press were buzzing Combe House. They had run out of rumours about the royal wedding and now needed to dig deeper for their daily fix. Everyone's life would be made a misery in the search for pictures and stories.

Especially mine, she thought with a chill of dread. Once the paparazzi arrived at a scene, everyone was fair game. The media feeding frenzy surrounding the Kahani wedding would need to be stoked every day. If there were no fresh details about the bride or groom, the circle would widen. Sooner or later, a slow news day would throw up Alyssa's name, and her part in Georgie's tragedy. It would be filed as a 'human interest' story, without any humanity at all. Her past pain would be raked over again, trapping her in a hell of her own making.

Lysander had proved he was the only one who could free her from that—and he was getting ready to marry someone else.

The succulent image of Alyssa in her sleek green swimming costume was a gift to the press. It went around the world in moments. Lysander, still deep in political arrangements, eyes tired from endless diplomatic discussions and smothered in yards of royal red tape, saw it and felt something break inside him.

Akil had nagged him for years about changing his wild ways. Lysander had never listened, and now he was glad he hadn't. It had taken only one night with Alyssa to upset his carefully crafted public image, and make him consider something beyond his body's prime reactions. Akil hadn't managed that in a lifetime of moaning. Lysander had been perfectly happy enjoying himself, with no thought for anybody else. There hadn't been room in his busy social life for conventional things like a wife and family. Considerations like that were for other people, not him.

Then Alyssa had walked into his life, and sent his perfectly regulated life haywire. In the long, restless hours since he'd abandoned her, he'd come to a decision. A lot had to change—and his own attitude was top of the list. Alyssa thought he cared more about his image than anything else. That might have been true before they met, but things had moved on for both of them since then.

At first Lysander had found the idea of ruling anything, much less a whole country, a bleak and lonely prospect. Watching Alyssa dealing with Ra'id had changed his thinking. He saw there must be give and take, but within limits. His head was beginning to tell him that being a royal needed two people who liked to be involved with others while staying aloof from them, and didn't mind hard work or long hours. His heart filled with the warm glow of certainty as he thought of the only person he needed and wanted to fill that special place by his side.

One sleepless night later, he had everything straight in his mind. When all the official communiqués were drafted and sent, and all the phone calls fielded, he called a press conference. He had never cared about what the media said about him in the past, but that was before he became the undisputed ruler of Rosara, until Ra'id came of age. It wasn't simply his own feelings he had to think about now. He needed to put on a good act for everybody today, and a spectacular show for the only person who really mattered to him.

When the meeting was all over, Lysander pumped the rebel leader's hand for the last time and walked away. He had achieved nearly all his objectives. Ra'id was safe from idiot rebel attack now the people of Rosara had a strong leader. Lysander was in command, and everyone was on his side. From this moment on he could go where he liked, and do what he wanted. Everything was within his power, but somewhere along the line glamorous bars and nightclubs had lost their appeal. When he looked back on his old life, it felt so shallow and incomplete. Happy it was behind him now, he didn't want to waste time wondering why or when he had started to think differently. A vital part of his future was missing, and he was going back to England to reclaim it.

Commandeering the nearest vehicle, he set off to find Alyssa.

The past week had been one of the worst of Alyssa's life, but it was about to be eclipsed in spectacular fashion. It was late. Time and again over the past few days she had tried to put away the memory of Lysander and his moonlit kisses, but it was no good. Nothing she could do was a big enough distraction to obliterate thoughts of him. They were fixed in her mind like a full-colour, life-sized photograph of the event. Right now she was standing in the shower, but torrents of water could not wash away the contrast between her paradise then, and her living hell now. Lysander's disdain for her must be ice-cold. It was a side of him he had kept hidden with soft words and careful promises while they were together, but he'd more than made up for it since then.

She came out of the bathroom still towelling her hair dry. Keying commands into a remote-control handset, she plunged her living room into darkness and sent its heavy velvet drapes scurrying apart. She was tired, and would normally have walked straight through to her bedroom. Tonight, though, something made her hesitate. She went over and looked out of the window instead.

Combe House was so isolated, the countryside outside was completely black. All that gloom beyond the windows reflected Alyssa's feelings exactly. She stared into it until her eyes became accustomed to the dark, and she could make out shapes on the horizon. The pillowy silhouettes of oak trees to the east would soon show some hope of morning. As she watched she noticed a single point of light in the distance. She couldn't see any other stars, and wondered if it was a planet— Venus, maybe. That was supposed to be the morning star, after all. She couldn't find it in her heart to really care. She wondered again how she could have wasted so much time grieving for the broken engagement that had brought her here in the first place. That pain had been nothing, compared to the agony of losing Lysander.

The trauma of seeing him with another woman would be too much, but she would never be able to avoid it. She couldn't hand in her notice—she had to stay here and care for Ra'id. What would happen to him if she resigned? It wasn't only her conscience talking, it was her heart. She really loved the little boy, and this Princess Peronelle hadn't treated him very well the first time they'd met. That was unlikely to change when she became Queen of Rosara, or, as Alyssa already thought of her, the Wicked Stepmother.

Letting her imagination sweep her away, Alyssa sighed. She picked up the pieces of shattered childhood dreams often enough in her line of work. Prissy Princess Peronelle would be all over Prince Lysander, leaving him no time for Ra'id. A woman like that might employ any kind of help, just to keep the little boy out of the happy couple's way. Alyssa shuddered every time she thought about what it could be like. At the very least, she'd have to wait and see whether the Wicked Stepmother really lived up to her name. Worst of all, the idea of betraying Lysander's trust in her held her captive. He had admired her attitude and her work before they slept together, and he had always wanted the best nanny in the world to look after his nephew. Lysander's high opinion of her work was something that would never change. She didn't want to destroy those feelings in him by nailing her broken heart to her sleeve. At the first sign of snivelling he would lose all respect for her, and she would feel the same way about herself.

As she dredged through all her unhappy thoughts

the distant bright light played hide and seek among the trees. Soon, it didn't seem so far away. She opened the French doors to get a better look and the sound of a low-flying plane flickered through the air. It grew louder, focused on that single bright point.

Suddenly Combe House burst into life. Every security light on the estate blazed. The plane swung around to approach the estate's private landing strip. As it slid sideways through the floodlight beams the royal blue and yellow crest of Rosara on its side told everyone that this wasn't a drill. It was the real thing. The Prince Regent had arrived.

Transfixed, Alyssa stood and watched the plane disappear beyond the lime trees in front of the house. Lysander was here at last. The urge to rush out, throw herself into his arms and thank him for getting back safely almost overwhelmed her. Only self-respect held her back. She had broken down in front of him once before, and look where *that* had led…

Gripping the window sill, she felt her palms dampen. With a snort of derision she dragged the curtains closed again and snapped on the light. The dazzle made her see sense. There could be any number of reasons why a plane of the king's air fleet might drop in. Lysander didn't have to be on-board. He had no reason to come here in person any more, when he could be lording it in the Rose Palace like every previous King of Rosara. He would have too much to do, preparing his stunning home for Princess Peronelle.

She shut her eyes. Her fury couldn't sustain itself when she was running on empty. For six days she had put on a brave face. Now all she wanted to do was crawl into bed, pull the covers over her head and stay there.

She didn't get as far as her bedroom. A thunderous rapping on the door of her apartment rattled her nerves as hard as it shook the windows.

'Alyssa?'

It was him. Lysander.

She thought about running into her room and locking the door. That wouldn't work. He sounded in a mood to come straight after her and, in any case, Alyssa suddenly realised she didn't want to run away. Facing him with what he had done to her and how he had betrayed her was the only way to fix this. All the rage fermenting inside her bubbled to the surface and wouldn't let her retreat. She marched over to the door and flung it open.

There he stood. Lysander. He looked magnificent in his uniform—and slightly out of breath. She glanced over towards the closed curtains so he wouldn't see what she was thinking. It was quite some way from the landing strip to the house. He must have sprinted all the way.

'I'm here to take you home, Alyssa.'

'What for? As your second-best woman?' she seethed. 'Sorry, you've come to the wrong place. Save the fairy tales for your nephew. I'm through believing in your stories.'

Her voice dripped acid as she tried—and failed—to slam the door in his face. It bounced off his boot as he kicked at the gap.

'I've spent the past week putting Ra'id's interests

first. It's you I'm interested in now, Alyssa. I've come for *you*.'

She froze. Lysander was a master of shock tactics, and used her momentary pause to wade straight into the attack. He spoke quickly, his chest rising and falling as though he didn't have time to catch his breath.

'You told me to go to hell—well, I've been there, and now I'm back. I've proved I can do my job better than any other man alive—'

'And now the Kahani inheritance is safe.'

'Yes.'

'How does it feel? Any better than turning your back on me at The Queen's Retreat?' Alyssa stared at him, very still apart from the crimson blush firing her cheeks.

'I had to do that.'

'Why? To prove you could?'

He turned all the power of his blazing eyes on her. After a long pause only fractured by his roughened breathing, his answer bruised the silence.

'Yes. Great empires have been brought down by women who weren't fit to look you in the face, Alyssa. It's happened in Rosara, too—twice in my lifetime. The first time it was my mother, the second time Akil's wife was the cause of all the trouble. I've never wanted to risk making the same mistakes other men in my family did. I needed to show the world—and myself—that I could put my country before my heart.'

'And what about *me*? What part are you expecting me to play in the Lysander Kahani Appreciation Society?' Alyssa forced the words past a growing lump in her throat.

'My people need strong leadership. Rosara has that now, and I must start building a team to take it into the future. I have to be the managing director of a whole country—'

'Or an engineer, calculating how to get rid of dead weight?' The chill in her voice reacted with his anger to make him hiss with exasperation.

'I came here to explain things to you, Alyssa. Can't you at least let me have my say?'

'I don't need explanations. I don't even want to *look* at you!' She turned her back so he wouldn't see her tears. 'You've got everything you want. Rosara, a fiancée hanging on your every word, and now you've come back to tie up the last inconvenient loose end—*me*!'

There was a pause. She heard him walk around so he could take up a position in front of her again. When she refused to raise her head, he bent down and looked up into her face. He was running his teeth over his bottom lip, perplexed. She closed her eyes to get him out of her sight. After an agony of silence, she heard him retreat.

'No...' he said eventually. 'I can't say I understood a word of that.'

'And I always thought your English was so perfect,' she snapped.

'Yes. It's about as good as your manners.'

The sound of him pacing backwards and forwards across her room was almost enough to make Alyssa open her eyes. Before she could gather the strength to do it, he started talking again.

'You're right about the loose ends, at least. It was unforgivable, shutting you out so completely. I had to force myself to do it. Alyssa, you were everything to me that night and while I've been away I've kept you close with every heartbeat. You're right—sending you back to England with Ra'id was partly a test. I had to know if I could carry on being everything to my country while you were affecting me so much. When we were together—when we made love, I forgot everything but you.' His voice became a whisper as he searched her face for any change in her feelings. 'That...frightened me. It was, after all, the same kind of madness that led to my father breaking down in tears every time my mother's name was mentioned.' A spasm of pain passed over his face. Shocked by the violence of his reaction, Alyssa automatically threw out her hands to him, but with a shake of his head he turned away.

'You've never dealt with that?' she whispered in horror.

He shook his head a second time, but still couldn't face her. 'Or the thought of how my brother was fooled by his ex-wife.'

Alyssa felt her heart hammer a warning against her ribs. Lysander was hurting, but then so was she. *He's gone from having a new woman every night to having a fiancée—and me*, she thought viciously. *Two pretty permanent fools, and both on strings.*

'So whatever made you turn to seduction as a career, Lysander? It sounds like you've grown to hate women over the years.'

'I don't hate them. I love them. But only on my own terms. I could never afford to let them get too close.' He looked at her then, biting his lip as though realising he had said the wrong thing.

Alyssa folded her arms as though that could protect her from him. 'I came here determined never to let you within a million miles of me, ever again,' she said, staring at him as the darkest pain of his past began to ebb from his expression. It was a moment of absolute stillness—until a huge crash made them both start and look back at the door connecting Alyssa's suite to the nursery.

'Alyssa! Come and hear what's on the radio—' Ra'id burst in, fresh out of bed and heading straight for her. Seeing Lysander, he squealed with delight and changed direction. Alyssa was already half crouching, ready to scoop the little boy up in her arms. As he threw himself at Lysander instead she slowly straightened up. Her original aim had been to see them happy together, but for the first time watching someone else's family bloom, without her, didn't ease her pain.

'Uncle Ly! You're on my radio, and you're here, too!' The little boy was jiggling up and down with excitement. Lysander was having trouble keeping hold of him, but neither of them seemed to care. They were both laughing. Alyssa took a step back, leaving them to enjoy themselves. This was family time. There was no room for a nanny at moments like this, but she had never given a second's thought to this part of her job before now. Now it hurt to know that Ra'id would always have a place in Lysander's heart, while she had none.

Lysander was getting his smartphone out of a pocket and holding it up to show Ra'id. 'Now I'm back, you don't need to listen to the radio. You can see what I've been saying to people on here.'

'It's me! Look, it's a picture of me!' Ra'id bellowed, grabbing Lysander's phone hand and wrenching it round so Alyssa could see the display, too. The little boy was focused on the one thing that meant anything to him, but that was only a small part of a much bigger picture. The phone showed film of Lysander, giving his last press conference in Rosara. Projected onto a screen behind him as he spoke was a photograph he must have taken during their last picnic. Alyssa was hugging Ra'id, and they were both in fits of laughter. As the camera moved away from the backdrop and zoomed in on Lysander's face Alyssa didn't know how much more she could take. She pushed her words past the blockage in her throat.

'Perhaps Your Majesty would like to put the prince back to bed himself?'

Ra'id put his arms around Lysander's neck as the successful conqueror nodded at her and set off towards the door connecting Alyssa's suite to the nursery.

'I'm coming back to carry on where we left off, Alyssa, right after I've put Ra'id back to bed,' he said firmly, disappearing into the bedroom and closing its door behind him.

Alyssa was so angry and emotionally exhausted she couldn't think what to do. She stood staring at the door blankly. When, after a long time, it opened again, she was alert to the smallest detail. Lysander locked the connecting door behind him to make sure they wouldn't be disturbed. Alyssa made a noise of disgust.

'Typical! I wonder how often you've done that in the past.'

'I've come back for you, Alyssa. What's wrong with that?'

'Because, like a fool, I let you seduce me despite the fact I've always known what you were like.'

Lysander said nothing to begin with, but she could tell he was angry. He betrayed it in the rigid set of his jaw and the iron intensity of his stare. It was a long time before he could trust himself to answer. He stood, trying to collect himself while her nerves stretched to breaking point.

'That's why you're different, Alyssa,' he said in a ragged voice. 'You've always seen the man in me, not the image.'

'Really? And which bit of you do all those women in all those glossy magazines get to enjoy?'

'What can I say?' He hitched a weary shoulder. 'I've told you—I like women. They like me.'

Alyssa's voice was carbon steel. 'I've noticed. I wonder how Princess Peronelle will feel about that.'

He looked at her askance. 'Why should *she* care?'

'When she's your wife, she'll do more than care. Be careful she doesn't stab you through that wicked black heart of yours, Lysander Kahani.'

His careful study became a frown. Alyssa's fists were balled, waiting for him to try something. What he did was so unexpected, she didn't have either the time or the sense to react. Taking her gently by the arm, he led her to the nearest chair. Putting his other hand to her forehead, he felt her temperature. She shook it off angrily.

'Don't do that to me!'

'I'm worried about you, Alyssa.'

'Oh, don't give me that! You sweet-talked me and seduced me in a moonlit garden, while all the time you were getting ready to make vows of undying love to another woman in the chapel of the Rose Palace!'

'Alyssa, you aren't making sense...' His refusal to come clean infuriated her.

'Yes, I am! I'm sick of making a fool of myself over you, when all the time I was nothing more than a stopgap until you married Princess Peronelle. Well, good luck to you both—and you'd better tell her not to bother running to me when you start tearing *her* heart to shreds!' Alyssa bounced out of her seat, her sense of injustice growing by the second. 'I'd rather have taken my chance in Rosara and been blown to bits a thousand times than watch you wreck another woman's life!'

He gazed at her with those steady dark eyes that had always spoken straight to her heart—until now.

'What in the hell are you talking about, Alyssa?'

'Don't give me that! You had the cold-blooded nerve to seduce me, when all along you knew you were lined up to marry Princess Peronelle!'

'Who told you that?'

'Ra'id. He said his father arranged everything, before he died.'

With that, all the weariness fell away from Lysander's face and he gave her a look of naked disbelief.

'You're not telling me you believed what a five-year-old boy told you? Or that I ever, in my entire life, did anything simply because my older brother thought it was a good idea?'

'Of course I believed it!' Alyssa exclaimed. 'It's all over the news! Everyone's been saying how King Akil picked you out the perfect bride, years ago. Ra'id just filled in the details for me.'

'That little monkey…' Lysander said in a slow, faint voice. 'Oh, Alyssa…my brother was always dreaming up schemes to make Rosara great. I didn't agree to a fraction of them when he was alive, and once he was dead I conveniently forgot the ones that didn't interest me. There has been so much more going on in my life since that was discussed. Time has passed, I had to come to terms with Akil's death while making sure Ra'id was well cared for, and then I had to get used to the idea of being Regent—an arranged marriage never crossed my mind. You didn't really think I'd be party to something like that, did you?'

'Of course I did.'

'But the whole idea is ridiculous! I've never given it a minute's consideration.' He put a hand over his eyes. 'Although I'm sure the people of Rosara thought there was nothing they'd like better than a royal wedding between me and Peronelle, until I told them in that press conference about something much more exciting.'

'Is that why you let the English-speaking media get away with printing all the details of your wedding, right down to who would be designing the bride's dress?'

He raised his hands to the sky. 'I have been fighting for my family's birthright. How the *hell* was I supposed to find the time to read newspapers?'

Alyssa felt her temperature heading off the scale again. 'You didn't need to—and neither did I. The press must have been following you everywhere. Didn't they say anything?'

Wearily raising his hands, Lysander went to cup

her face. She took a step back. Fury flared in his face. His arms shot out and he caught her by the shoulders. Pulling her close, he trapped her body as well as her gaze.

'My mind has been full of other things. I've told you—I've been too distracted to care about rumours, tales and lies.'

'It was a shame *I* couldn't manage to distract you better than I did.' Alyssa's words crackled like static.

So far, Lysander had been on the defensive. Her accusation changed everything.

'For one brief moment in my country's history, you were far more distraction than I could handle. I thought the pleasure you brought me would dilute my sense of duty. It was only when I managed to put some distance between us, I could get things into perspective.' He hesitated, and looked almost embarrassed as he added quietly, 'Things like...the way I feel about you.'

'That I was a handy stand-in until your honeymoon with Peronelle?'

Alyssa's granite stare was as abrasive as her words. She couldn't risk falling for his lies a second time.

'Oh, Alyssa! When you and I... What *do* you think I am? Doesn't the fact that I came back to fetch you home prove that you mean more to me than any other woman in my life? You're the only one who really matters to me, Alyssa,' he said simply.

Alyssa wanted to believe him, but there was something that didn't quite fit. 'You said there's only one thing your people would enjoy more than a royal wedding. You never said what it was.'

'A love match, of course. So that's what I'm going to give them.'

He sounded as cool and resolute as he had on the day when he had abandoned her in Rosara. For good or bad, his mind was made up about something. Alyssa had to know his decision and who was involved, but she hesitated. Did she really want to know the name of her rival? It would be an unendurable pain, but surely it would be better to hear it from him, rather than at second hand.

'Who with?'

'You, of course.'

From the moment Lysander had walked into her suite she had matched him verbally, blow for blow. Now his words silenced her completely. He had befriended her, helped her—and then inflicted a wound so deep she knew she would never recover. Only the furious memory of the way he had bundled her out of Rosara had got her this far. Now a growing anger at her own idiocy kept her staring straight at him. She had always known he would never marry her. If he was offering her a taste of what might have been, she would have to refuse. She couldn't agree to be his mistress, kept as first reserve until next year's model dazzled him into dropping her. That was what he was offering, surely. She wasn't worth anything more—all her experiences showed that. She had to drive him away, quickly, before she succumbed.

'Check your schedule, Your Majesty. You're already pencilled in to marry Princess Peronelle at the Kahani chapel, in six weeks' time.' She spat the words straight into his face, but he didn't blink.

'Then hand me an eraser. I want you.'

'Yes, but everybody knows you need a suitable wife.'

'I don't care what "everybody knows", and I don't want a wife, suitable or otherwise. I want a partner—someone who knows my mind. An intelligent, independent, thinking woman I can work with.'

His stare was as hard and resolute as his words. They confronted each other until the tension began to have a very strange effect on Alyssa. In her imagination she saw his eyelids flicker. His jaw relaxed, and the thin compressed line of his lips softened with the movement. He spoke, and that was when Alyssa knew she must be dreaming.

'I want *you*,' he repeated, and this time there could be no doubt about it. 'That's what I told everyone at the press conference. That's why Ra'id heard me talking about a queen. You're the only one I want at my side, Alyssa.'

They stared at each other, each determined not to give in. Alyssa blinked first, and it gave Lysander the break he had been waiting for. He added something, but had to turn away to say it. His voice was so faint Alyssa could barely hear, but the movement of his beautiful mouth gave him away.

There were only two words she could fit to those faint sounds, and they were so unlikely the idea kick-started her own voice.

'*What* did you just say?' she breathed. He slowly turned around and seized her hands in his, his eyes blazing into hers with dark emotion.

'Marry me.'

Lysander's voice was uncompromising. It was an

order, not a request, but in his eyes there was a flicker of something that took her breath away. Surely not, but it looked as if he was…nervous? Alyssa felt dizzy, as though the ground had suddenly been turned upside down.

'Lysander! But…I can't…' Half a dozen reasons dug their spiteful claws into her, but they were all variations on the same theme. 'You rule Rosara. I'm a nanny.'

'Do you think I care about that?'

'You should.' Alyssa took a deep breath, hardly able to believe what was happening. 'I want to marry you more than anything else in the world. But you know what my problem is. I want children, and a family— all the things you've spent your life avoiding. I want to keep working. And how could I go on doing that, when I'm married to you? Without my job, without caring, I'm nothing.'

Lysander's grip became gentler.

'You could never be a woman defined only by the work she does, Alyssa. Don't you think I've thought about that? Care for me. For Ra'id and, in time, for our own children. You'll be the perfect, dedicated mother, and that's one of the reasons I love you.'

He coloured slightly and his reply momentarily shocked Alyssa into speechlessness. She had never imagined Lysander using a four-letter word like love. Now his country was safe, it seemed it wasn't only his lifestyle that was changing.

'I never knew you could blush, Lysander!'

He passed one hand over his face, then looked down at her as resolutely as ever. 'It isn't something I intend doing a second time. And I'm not likely to repeat what I've just said, either.'

Alyssa felt a smile start to spread across her face. He was searching her face, his expression earnest. 'I want you to work *with* me, not simply *for* me. Children are our future, Alyssa, whichever way you look at it. Ra'id needs a settled, loving home life. I want him to live with us, as our son. In your spare time—if he gives you any—Rosara needs someone who understands that the care our children get decides our country's future. You can be their champion.'

He paused, but it was Alyssa who had to take a breath. The look in his eyes had softened to melting chocolate.

'I need a woman by my side I can rely on—one who can help me achieve all I want to do. So this time I'm not so much presenting you with a job, as asking you to work with me. For life.' His eyes blazed with a certainty Alyssa couldn't face. She had to look away.

'You know I'll never be a Princess Peronelle, don't you? With me, what you see is what you get,' she said quietly.

Relief flooded his face, and he smiled for the first time. 'I know. That's why we'll be happy together. You'll carry on being the independent woman who always tells me what she thinks and only laughs at my jokes if they're funny, and that's exactly what I want—and need. So…what's your answer going to be? Could you take us on? Me and my world?'

Alyssa looked up at the ceiling, pretending to think.

'Hmm. Well, knowing you, if I don't accept we'll be here all night arguing…so I suppose I'll have to say—yes!' She laughed up at him, loving the way his eyes had lit up with joy. 'Of course, you'll have to dismantle the rumour machine and survive telling Princess Peronelle the fixture's scratched, first.'

'I don't intend telling anybody anything, for a very long time.' Catching her hand, he pulled it to his lips and kissed each of her fingertips in turn. 'Unless it's you, Alyssa.'

His eyes were full of the slow-burning passion she knew so well, but tonight it was misted with deep emotion. Slipping her arms around his waist, she laid her head against his chest.

'So you'll be disappointing all those supermodels as well as the princess, then?'

'I'd rather satisfy you.' He laughed. And then he did—perfectly.

* * * * *

Mills & Boon® Hard Back

October 2011

ROMANCE

The Most Coveted Prize	Penny Jordan
The Costarella Conquest	Emma Darcy
The Night that Changed Everything	Anne McAllister
Craving the Forbidden	India Grey
The Lost Wife	Maggie Cox
Heiress Behind the Headlines	Caitlin Crews
Weight of the Crown	Christina Hollis
Innocent in the Ivory Tower	Lucy Ellis
Flirting With Intent	Kelly Hunter
A Moment on the Lips	Kate Hardy
Her Italian Soldier	Rebecca Winters
The Lonesome Rancher	Patricia Thayer
Nikki and the Lone Wolf	Marion Lennox
Mardie and the City Surgeon	Marion Lennox
Bridesmaid Says, 'I Do!'	Barbara Hannay
The Princess Test	Shirley Jump
Breaking Her No-Dates Rule	Emily Forbes
Waking Up With Dr Off-Limits	Amy Andrews

HISTORICAL

The Lady Forfeits	Carole Mortimer
Valiant Soldier, Beautiful Enemy	Diane Gaston
Winning the War Hero's Heart	Mary Nichols
Hostage Bride	Anne Herries

MEDICAL ROMANCE™

Tempted by Dr Daisy	Caroline Anderson
The Fiancée He Can't Forget	Caroline Anderson
A Cotswold Christmas Bride	Joanna Neil
All She Wants For Christmas	Annie Claydon

Mills & Boon® Large Print

October 2011

ROMANCE

Passion and the Prince — Penny Jordan

For Duty's Sake — Lucy Monroe

Alessandro's Prize — Helen Bianchin

Mr and Mischief — Kate Hewitt

Her Desert Prince — Rebecca Winters

The Boss's Surprise Son — Teresa Carpenter

Ordinary Girl in a Tiara — Jessica Hart

Tempted by Trouble — Liz Fielding

HISTORICAL

Secret Life of a Scandalous Debutante — Bronwyn Scott

One Illicit Night — Sophia James

The Governess and the Sheikh — Marguerite Kaye

Pirate's Daughter, Rebel Wife — June Francis

MEDICAL ROMANCE™

Taming Dr Tempest — Meredith Webber

The Doctor and the Debutante — Anne Fraser

The Honourable Maverick — Alison Roberts

The Unsung Hero — Alison Roberts

St Piran's: The Fireman and Nurse Loveday — Kate Hardy

From Brooding Boss to Adoring Dad — Dianne Drake

ROMANCE

The Power of Vasilii	Penny Jordan
The Real Rio D'Aquila	Sandra Marton
A Shameful Consequence	Carol Marinelli
A Dangerous Infatuation	Chantelle Shaw
Kholodov's Last Mistress	Kate Hewitt
His Christmas Acquisition	Cathy Williams
The Argentine's Price	Maisey Yates
Captive but Forbidden	Lynn Raye Harris
On the First Night of Christmas...	Heidi Rice
The Power and the Glory	Kimberly Lang
How a Cowboy Stole Her Heart	Donna Alward
Tall, Dark, Texas Ranger	Patricia Thayer
The Secretary's Secret	Michelle Douglas
Rodeo Daddy	Soraya Lane
The Boy is Back in Town	Nina Harrington
Confessions of a Girl-Next-Door	Jackie Braun
Mistletoe, Midwife...Miracle Baby	Anne Fraser
Dynamite Doc or Christmas Dad?	Marion Lennox

HISTORICAL

The Lady Confesses	Carole Mortimer
The Dangerous Lord Darrington	Sarah Mallory
The Unconventional Maiden	June Francis
Her Battle-Scarred Knight	Meriel Fuller

MEDICAL ROMANCE™

The Child Who Rescued Christmas	Jessica Matthews
Firefighter With A Frozen Heart	Dianne Drake
How to Save a Marriage in a Million	Leonie Knight
Swallowbrook's Winter Bride	Abigail Gordon

Mills & Boon® Large Print

November 2011

ROMANCE

HISTORICAL

MEDICAL ROMANCE™